THE
EIDOLON

K.D. EDWARDS

A TALE FROM NEW ATLANTIS

ISBN-13: 979-8-9874287-2-6

Front Cover art by Bethany Cath
Rear Cover art by Dezaray Shuler
Full Cover design by Justyna Chlopecka and XM Moon
Internal typesetting and design by XM Moon
Arcanum Seal by Jake Shandy
Map design by Rowan Danckert

For more information, including content warnings, please visit kd-edwards.com/extra-content

For my Beta Readers, who helped get this book to the finish line, and reminded me how lucky I am to have the type of readers and friends I do.

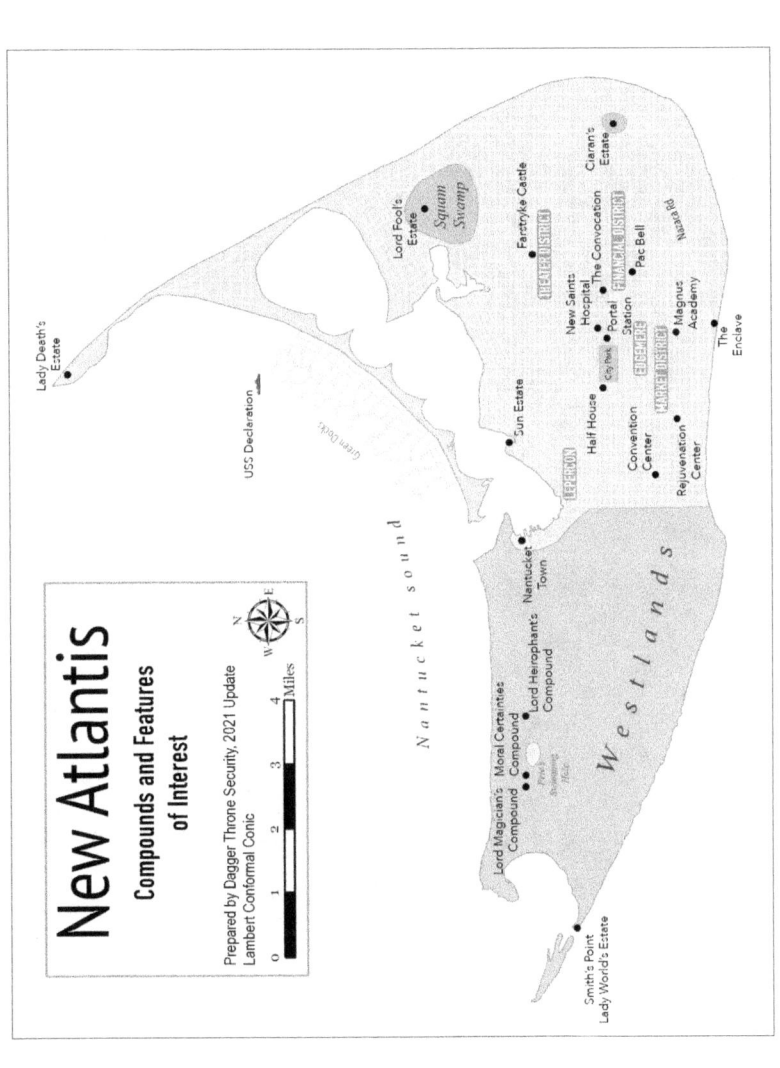

TABLE OF CONTENTS

FOREWORD

Putting together *The Eidolon* was the chance of a lifetime.

Traditional publishing has its drawbacks. A strict limit to the page count of the third book in my main series, *The Tarot Sequence*, forced me to cut a significant storyline about my "book kids" – the younger generation of Sun Estate.

The problem was that this excised material was big. Really big. Fundamentally important things happen to Max, Quinn, and Anna—especially in the Epilogue—that will change readers' perspective of *everything* that's come before this. So I set about drafting the idea for a standalone novella that told their story. While I've billed this book as being the start of a Magnus Academy series, it really has its foot in two worlds: as an extension of *Hourglass* (and book 3.5 of the main *TAROT* series), and as a novel fully built around the teens, who might become the main characters of a Magnus Academy series.

Things snowballed from there. The novella became—technically, at least—a short novel. Not only did I get to expand my vision of the mysterious ghost trap called the Eidolon, I was able to include more scenes with the villainous Lady Jade. I was able to include characters tangentially referenced in the main series who were never described on paper before. I also saved one of my biggest "series bombs" for the story—including a scene that I've waited years to write, which will give *The Eidolon* readers advance notice on certain revelations bearing down on Rune in the next two main books.

Even better? I opted for a hybrid publishing model for this short novel. A limited-edition hardcover was prepared by the queer subscription book service, Rainbow Crate. Audible produced an audiobook. And I sell a modestly priced eBook, and also this paperback, now.

This turned out to be a phenomenally positive endeavor. Working with Rainbow Crate was an author's dream. They actively sought more content, so we added interior art, a glossary, a map, an author's foreword... This is all in addition to making the gift edition a very high-quality printing project.

In a way, reading this story will make you a prophet. You'll learn things that Rune doesn't know. And while the next two books, *The Misfit Caravan* and *The Exiled Courts*, will inevitably lead to Rune learning these secrets, I like making you conspirators with me.

For those of you who'd like to know how the pacing of *The Eidolon* overlaps with *The Hourglass Throne*, here's my personal cheat guide:

THE EIDOLON CHAPTER NUMBER – TO – THE HOURGLASS THRONE CHAPTER NAME

Prologue – Before "The Principality Ciaran"

Chapter 1 – Simultaneously with "The Gala"

Chapter 2 – Simultaneously with "The Manse"

Chapter 3 – After "The Manse"

Chapter 4 – After "The Manse"

Chapter 5 – After "The Manse"

Chapter 6 – Simultaneously with "The Arcanum"

Chapter 7 – Simultaneously with "The Revelry"

Chapter 8 – Simultaneously with "The Revelry"

Chapter 9 – Simultaneously with "The Revelry"

Chapter 10 – After "The Warrens"

Chapter 11 – Simultaneously with "Half House"

Endgame – Simultaneously with "Farstryke"

Epilogue – Simultaneously with "Epilogue"

This world I've created is the work of a lifetime. I will happily playing in this sandbox until I lay down my pen. Thank you so much for exploring this entirely new facet of the Tarot universe with me. I appreciate all of you so much.

KD, 9/24/25

PROLOGUE
Quinn

The wheel on the oxygen cart squealed as Quinn dragged it across the small stretch of grass that led to a downtown plaza.

There was no oxygen cylinder in it, just an assortment of random objects, including an umbrella, a rake, several plywood boards, and a plastic bag of quarters, dimes, and nickels. He'd found the cart in the basement of Sun Estate and gladly traded his heavy duffle bag for it.

The first few stops were easy.

He left a dollar and eighty-five cents in one of the city's rare remaining payphones. The umbrella went behind the bench of an unsheltered bus stop outside a women's shelter. The boards were carefully laid down on a sewer grate.

He would squint in the air and chew his lip every so often. Slowly, the things he Saw stopped spinning in so many chaotic directions. The nice lady almost always never tripped; the young woman usually grabbed the umbrella and sat quietly in the rain until she found the resolve to cross the road; and the penniless man with the tears in his eyes usually called the American embassy before something hunted him down. (It was unclear what *something* was, but the man wrote a really pretty song in the future, and Quinn wanted a copy for his playlist.)

He turned his gnawed lip to the rake, trying to remember where that one went. He suspected he had a walk ahead of him.

Before he could settle on a direction, he saw a white-haired boy across the road and sucked in a breath. Was this when Max found him?

He exhaled. *No.* First, it wasn't Max; and second, not-Max was in front of a hot pretzel stand, and Quinn was certain he would have remembered that.

Stomach growling, he took a left and squeaked his way toward the city's financial district. The rake wanted to go there. He still wasn't entirely sure *where* amidst the office buildings, or *why*, but money did strange things to people. The air in those blocks had the slick, humming energy of a rush hour ATM dispenser.

He caught a second glimpse of white-blond hair moving into a cafe, but this was another not-Max, because Max hated plain white tee shirts. Plus, this close to *actually happening*, Quinn was sure Max wouldn't be easily spotted. He'd been practicing his stealth skills lately and almost always tried to spook Quinn. So Quinn practiced a surprised face for a few seconds, which seemed polite.

Then he got distracted by the fountain in the middle of the plaza he was about to cross.

The futures sang, a whiplash of images backed by the omnipresent, heart-muffled thudding of magic. His images always sounded like whitewater rapids.

He didn't like everything he was seeing, but there was a dog involved, and he was a sucker for dogs and cats. He dragged the oxygen cart to the rim of the fountain, took off his shoes and socks, and waded into the shallow water. Metal coins slid under his feet as he sloshed to the big stone monument in the middle of the water, like a totem pole with random hands sticking out of it. At the top was a weathervane.

He gently climbed the hands—trying not to wince as onlookers gave him the side-eye—and used a wad of grape chewing gum to fix the weathervane in the East position.

That was where both Max and the guarda officer found him. They literally approached the fountain at the same time from opposite directions, and the futures that spun from that moment required so much tiresome explanation.

"I'll handle this," Max told the guarda, using what Quinn liked to call Max's Scion Voice.

The man in the green and amber uniform was not impressed. Shoulders squared, he began to advance, but Max lazily swiped up his sleeve to show a round flame emblem on his forearm.

It *looked* like an Arcana seal, if an Arcana seal was made of wax, markers, and some tricky cantrip magic that Max and Anna had cooked up on the sly. Max got the idea from Ciaran, who seemed to sprout Arcana seals whenever he needed them.

Fortunately, Max flashed it quickly enough to obscure both the seal's basement-workshop origin and the fact that the red marker smelled like cherries.

Max said, "I'm Matthias Saint John, brother to Lord Sun. I'll take care of this."

The officer flicked a dubious gaze to Quinn, then back to Max. "He's coming out of the water, right?"

"This very moment," Max promised.

"My lord," the officer said and, neck bowed, left them alone before he got sucked into business above his pay grade.

"The dog was glowing, it's not my fault," Quinn said to Max's wide-armed what-the-hell gesture. "He was like a little bonfire. And he's a very good boy, too."

"A glowing dog made you climb to the top of a fountain?"

"Well, no, the weathervane made me climb. I think there's a really superstitious man? He doesn't like the fact that the wind is blowing from the west. So now he doesn't make a stupid decision and lives to have a puppy, and the puppy grows into an important glowing dog. Do you have any handkerchiefs on you?"

"No, Quinn. I do not have any handkerchiefs on me. You're out here saving a man's life?"

"Meh," Quinn muttered, climbing off the last granite hand. His feet sunk back into the cold water. "His futures are all mustard and ochre. I don't think I'd like him very much. I like the dog."

Max held out his hand to help—well, drag—Quinn over the lip of the fountain. He had the look on his face that he'd unconsciously stolen from Rune—the one where he was putting pieces together, and every single one of those guesses was molding his expression like a movie subtitle.

"Do we have anything to do with the man?" Max finally asked. "Or the dog?"

Quinn pretended to be busy finding another piece of chewing gum. "Not really."

Max stared at the weathervane, then dropped his gaze to the oxygen cart. He poked at the bag of spare change. Studied the rake.

"What," he said, "are you doing, Quinn? Is this what you've been doing all those times you sneak out?"

"I do not sneak," Quinn said. "I just… leave. For a walk."

"Do you use your gifts to help you find the best path to walk off the estate that doesn't involve bumping into anyone?" Max asked.

He is getting so good at asking questions, Quinn thought. He popped the gum in his mouth and pointed apologetically to his moving jaw.

"Because if you're using your prophecy to find a route off the estate, that's sneaking. That is literally sneaking. Are you… What, practicing? Is this about using your prophecy and getting better at it?"

There wasn't enough grape flavor in the world to outlast Max's insistence. Quinn sighed through a bubble, sat down, and began putting his socks back on.

"Maybe," he said. "Ever since the battleship, when my powers got super-charged for a while, my visions are getting… stronger."

"Okay. So, you *are* practicing your powers?" Max asked.

Quinn didn't want to answer that because he was soaring close to the hard, clear line of a lie. And he had no intention of telling Max that it wasn't what he *saw* that was the problem. It's what he *wasn't* seeing.

How did you tell people you love that you weren't seeing futures anymore with you in them?

"I just like helping people," Quinn said, with the most earnest expression in his emotional toolbox.

Max stared hard at him.

"We should get back to the estate," Quinn added. "We've got that fitting for our coronation outfits."

CHAPTER ONE
Quinn

A day later, Anna was nearly stabbed to death, and Rune had a now-healed hole burned through him. The attack had been sudden and unexpected, exploding into Quinn's perception barely seconds before the warning would have come too late.

It shook him. Rarely had his gift so thoroughly let him down. One second, he was standing by Flynn's paddock as Rune talked with some annoying scion visitor, the next he saw the attack—images of violence dissolving under a slick, corrosive film.

Rune and Brand stopped the attack. Anna and Rune were healed. And then the same exact attack happened at two more Arcana courts over the following days.

Quinn was getting itchier and itchier. Something big was bearing down on them—any one of the big, horrible things crouched behind Rune's long horizon. Anna and Rune had become bonfires of possibilities—thick, big, loud futures howling in every direction. It hurt to look at them, these days.

The attacks had happened not long after dozens of people were murdered at Lady Priestess's Rejuvenation Center, which had caused Brand and Rune to do a lot of whispering. Max and Quinn got nosy and poked into it, which is why they had a sketch of the murder suspect. Max had taken a picture of the drawing from Rune's file, and the two teens were now trying to help on the sly. Since they were good at research, they'd been doing reverse facial recognition searches to see if they could find images of her in newspapers or social media.

And then, all too soon, the day of Rune's coronation was upon them.

"Rune said we could have a glass of wine every ninety minutes," Max whispered, rubbing his hands together. "I love asking Rune for permission."

"I don't think I want any wine," Quinn said.

"Well, come with me to get one," Max told him, and dragged Quinn toward one of the bars on the lower tiers of the lawn, far away from the particular area set aside for the Sun Throne and its people.

Rune's coronation gala was being hosted by Lady Death at her estate on the northeastern peninsula. That was nice. Quinn was thrilled to be friends with her finally. Sometimes it didn't happen for years and years, but Rune had a knack for speeding timelines up. Now they were almost on a first-name basis, which was one of the safest threads in Rune's many possible lives. And the only threads Quinn watched more closely than Addam's were the ones belonging to Rune and Anna. Especially Rune, because Rune was, and always had been, the small hub at the heart of a gigantic spider's web. So many strands spun around him.

"What is *wrong* with you?" Max complained.

"Can I see the sketch again?" Quinn evaded.

But they were at the bar, so Max turned into Matthias. Straight-backed, broad-shouldered, a pretty face rapidly aging into handsome.

"I would like a glass of red wine in the largest cup you have available," Max said politely. "No—not that one. I'll take the sixteen-ounce tumbler." In a side hiss, he said, "Can I borrow money for a tip?"

"I guess?" Quinn said.

Max, much to Quinn's surprise, pulled Quinn's wallet out

of his own pocket, took the wine, and left behind a ten.

"It's just," Quinn said as they walked away from the bar, "it doesn't feel like borrowing when you already have my money."

Max smacked his lips after taking a long, bitter sip. "First of all, Lord Moral High Ground, I think you're going to feel pretty awful when you remember you always forget your wallet, and I'm always having to grab it for you."

"Oh," Quinn said. "I do do that a lot, don't I?"

"And second," Max continued, "I'll airdrop the sketch. Why do you keep staring at it?"

"Just because," Quinn murmured. His phone vibrated. He pulled it out and accepted the airdrop Max had sent from his phone. Quinn opened the drawing and stared at the heavily lined face. It was surreal seeing an Atlantean that old.

"I'm going to grab some stuffed mushrooms," Max said. "Be right back."

Barely a second had passed before Quinn's mother approached him. She was in a conversation with one of her husbands, who left to fetch whatever she asked for. She passed near Quinn without a glance, not seeing his cheery wave.

He sighed, but it wasn't an accusation. He didn't blame her. He knew she could change. When you could See ahead and know that a person could really and truly change, it gave your hope extra gas.

Max came back with an actual platter with only a few mushrooms left on it. He also came back drunker.

The two of them munched on their snack and made their way back to the VIP tier. Max insisted on keeping close to the leafy bushes on the edge, so that Brand wouldn't spot the sixteen-ounce plastic cup and take it away from him. Max also mumbled about avoiding Anna so she didn't tell, which was unfair. Anna didn't usually bother tattling on people. She held a deep-seated belief that stupid people messed up on their own, and she'd made it clear that teenaged boys were stupid.

Was Quinn being stupid? Was it stupid not to find Addam right now, right now, and tell him that the futures were crawling across his skin like ants, and he couldn't see where he stood in them, or even whether he was standing at all? It was almost painful, this sense of impending—

And then, as with life, the apprehension of dread dissolved in the face of dread's final arrival.

Rune was dancing.

There was a small, cordoned square of grass for dancers, and Rune was dancing with an old woman in green. In *jade*.

Quinn lost control of his power.

It spiraled from him with hurricane arms—invisible lashings of prophecy and prediction, only what he saw was so much darker than usual. So much pain and defeat and despair. *That woman will put peanut oil in her husband's food*, he thought, *and that child stabs doll eyes. That man buries his neighbor's dog. The woman in a flowered dress will knit socks for her stillborn grandson.*

Worse. Darker and worse. The gala, unseen to everyone but him, swarmed with deadly predictions—*swarmed* with them, fruit flies on a rotting orange peel. Quinn could barely see the motions of people through the thick stream of infinities spinning outwards. They were just formless masses of death—people drowning in waves as tall as buildings; people lost under the stampede of hooves the size of church bells; people screaming as the skin was scoured from their throats.

Quinn used all his willpower to corral his gift. It was too much, though. He pivoted, ran to a bush, and threw up. Max was at his side a beat later.

"Did you have wine too?" Max asked, confused.

"What should we do?" Quinn whispered. "We should find Brand. Or Lord Tower. Where's Addam?"

"Find them why? Why are you throwing up? Now your nose is bleeding."

Quinn dabbed at his nose with the back of his wrist, a familiar, tiresome gesture. It wasn't a bad bleed. "I'm going to talk with Brand."

"He's right over there," Max said. He pulled out a square of cloth and gave it to Quinn.

Something about that touched Quinn. Quinn asked for a handkerchief one day, and suddenly Max was carrying handkerchiefs the next. *We used to argue over who was Rune and who was Brand.* It had been obvious from the start who was who, really.

"Max, listen to me," Quinn said, and urgency crept into his voice. "We'll find Brand. Don't do anything until we do. This isn't our fight—it can't be. Promise me."

"What are you on about? What is happening? Did you See something?"

"I see *her*," Quinn said and pointed toward the woman in jade behind a cupped palm.

"The woman Rune is dancing with?" Max said.

"The woman in green. In *jade*."

Max's eyes slid in that direction, and just as calmly slid back to Quinn. "Are you sure you aren't drinking wine?"

"Tell me you won't go after her. Tell me now, Max. Right now. Three times."

"Quinn," Max said in surprise.

Quinn had never asked anyone for a vow before. But there were so many threads where Max skated ahead of everyone and tried to land the first blow. Quinn would not let that happen.

"Tell me," Quinn said. "*Say it.*"

"Fine. I won't, I won't, I won't. What is *up* with you?"

There was no sense of rushing wind, the way there was when Rune made a vow. But Rune was Rune.

Quinn didn't have time to waste. He crossed along the far periphery of the dancing area to where Brand stood—and Addam, too, not far away. Max followed indulgently, though worry seemed to be eating into his buzz.

"Brand," Quinn whispered when they were close. "What should we do?"

Brand's eyes were on Rune. He darted a glance to Quinn

and then back to his lifelong charge. "I see Max hiding that cup. I'm only letting you pull this tricky shit because it's a special day."

"What do we do about *her*," Quinn said anxiously.

"Her who?"

"The woman in jade," Quinn said.

"She's a good dancer, isn't she? We should take a picture of her and Rune."

The complete lack of guile on Brand's face punctured Quinn's urgency and replaced the slow leak with another emotion: fear. "Can you see her?" he whispered. "Can you not..."

Quinn caught Rune's eyes. For just a moment, he caught Rune's eyes. Rune's completely baffling, dazed smile seemed to falter—and then he was caught back in the dance with a serial murderer.

The music ended moments later, and Rune was left alone in the middle of the grass square. He had a hand pressed against his lip. Brand, shaking his head like a dog hearing a distant whistle, followed Rune, who seemed to be looking around for a napkin.

Addam stepped around the people between him and Quinn. He laid a gentle hand on his younger brother's shoulder. "What is it?" he whispered.

"What is that woman wearing? The one walking away from Rune?" Quinn stared hard into his brother's burgundy eyes.

"A gown...?"

"What color?"

"Green, Quinn. What is this?"

"It's *jade*. She's wearing a *jade gown*. What does that mean to you, Addam?"

"I am not entirely sure. Do you like jade? Is this a gift hint?"

Quinn looked over at Rune and Brand, but now they were talking with someone else. He jiggled his weight from one foot to another, upset. He needed to speak with Rune. He had... a suspicion. It wasn't a good one. There were some threads he never looked at too closely.

Rune and Brand began to move away from the bar with the man—Vadik. Vadik Amberson. Quinn had met him just before the attack at Sun Estate, where Anna and Rune had been hurt.

Quinn told Addam he needed to go to the bathroom and followed them.

Twenty minutes later, he sat down at a table by himself, stunned. Not even talking to Rune had made a dent in whatever magic was at work. The only thing keeping Quinn from entirely losing his cool was that there'd been no actual violence yet.

Who was this woman? Why could no one see her?

Quinn knew bad things lay ahead. Some worse than others, some more likely, some less. He didn't see the shape of this emergency yet, but if it was tied to him not seeing his future anymore, then…

Well, then, this was one of the big ones. He said a quiet prayer of thanks that at least there weren't dragons in the sky. He'd gladly toss *that* potential future onto the shoulders of a Quinn in another timeline.

He also knew that the best course of action was inaction. The wrong word at the wrong time would send too many vibrations into the houses of cards he'd built to keep his family safe. He would watch and wait and hope he recognized the Moment he'd need to act before he stared down the barrel of its real, indelible seconds.

Max sat down next to him. His tumbler was freshly filled, and he'd found a smaller wine glass for Quinn. "You look like you need it," he said, though the *you* sounded like *yoush*.

Quinn gave the idea of wine a mental shrug and slid the glass closer to himself.

"Are you alright?" Max asked, and sober worry flickered

through his eyes.

"I think we should just… walk around, Max. And look for anything strange."

"Have you seen anything strange?" Max asked.

Quinn stared hard into his eyes, but it was useless. Any sense of danger just seemed to skitter away from Max's perception. "Brand would be impressed if we kept an eye on everyone while they're doing their diplomatic thing."

"Can we drink more wine while we watch?"

"Would you even let me take it away from you?"

"I'd let you try," he said and smiled.

So they walked around for a while. At one point, just for a moment, his clairvoyant gifts rustled and preened and put him into a trance. He felt a real, tiny, ferret-sized heart inside the nearby Manse—a fiery little supernova of prophecy. Quinn shook off the fugue and said, in a whisper, "Hey you. Do we meet already? I'm going to be very firm about some of the decisions you make, but I think we'll be okay."

"You are *so extra weird* today," Max exhaled. "Should we go talk with Addam?"

But that was when Aunt Diana rounded them up for Rune's big speech. And seeing his aunt, Quinn felt a little better, because more and more was going right. Wasn't it? His aunt was part of their family again. She was a very, very strong magic user. She made his house of cards that much firmer.

They were seated closest to the podium, which the Tower was leading Rune toward. Max and Quinn kept their wine carefully positioned in the shade of a large centerpiece, just outside the periphery of Addam's roving eye, which was easy enough, because Addam barely went seconds without snapping his gaze back to Rune.

At the podium, Rune was reaching for his pocket.

A sudden surge of magic moved across the gathering like a freight train. It was that quick. Powerful as a mass sigil spell, but infinitely more complex, magic washed over the lawn and froze everyone in place. *Quinn* was frozen—one hand on the table, half-risen from his chair.

There was a war in his brain—the magic felt like a glacier threatening to slide over his consciousness. His own power rose unbidden to his need, a flashfire that kept the freeze at bay. Perspiration trickled from his forehead, and he felt a single drop of blood snake down to his upper lip.

He didn't know what type of magic this was, but—

Oh yes you do, you do, you do, his brain whispered to him.

Terrified, Quinn could only stare through his motionless head at the single cone of vision in front of him.

The woman—Lady Jade—walked calmly up to the podium and beat Rune's paralyzed fingers to his pocket. She unfolded a piece of paper and read it while walking back away from the stand.

Right toward Quinn.

Rune's eyes did not follow her. No one's did. Was anyone seeing this? Where was the Tower? Where was Judgment? Quinn's head was fixed in a different direction than Addam's. Not being able to see his brother was maybe the scariest thing of all.

Lady Jade stopped in front of him. She pursed lips painted pale green.

"You're watching me," she said in a marveling tone. "You are actually watching me, aren't you, little Seer?"

She came so close to Quinn that she could bend and sniff his neck. When she spoke, her breath raised his flesh.

She said, "You break all the models, don't you? You build the roads people follow. And I cannot have that. You are not a piece I can allow on this game board."

She reached up and touched his chin. He could feel it— feel a calloused finger and the tip of the shiny, sharp nail.

"But do not worry," she said. "Blood like yours must not be lost. I will afford you all due rights under the old nobility laws for prisoners. This is my only offer to you. Come to me willingly, and you will be protected. But if I have to find you... Let us just say I can find ways to painfully contain you and preserve your bloodline. For instance, if I am correct, that is your brother over there, is it not? If you need more motivation, I could put my fist through his chest and pin his heart to your sleeve."

She didn't need an answer. She just smiled and said, "Midnight. If you're as good as I think, you'll find my people where they are waiting for you. Do we have a deal?"

She didn't move or make a gesture, but Quinn felt a small surge of magic, and his paralysis vanished.

He collapsed into his chair. His legs shook so badly he wouldn't have been able to stand if he wanted.

"Do we have a deal?" she repeated.

"Yes," he said hoarsely.

"Yes *who?* Who am I, little Seer? Say. My. Name."

And oh, he knew. He knew. He knew.

Quinn couldn't remember a period when he didn't know this would happen, even if he didn't know when. The inevitability had been cemented before Quinn was even born. He hadn't always known who it would be—a man or a woman, tall or short, pretty or scary—but he'd seen *this*, the return of *this* power.

"Time," he said. "You are Time. The Hourglass Throne has returned."

Her smile was a grim reward. She turned and walked away.

Across the clearing, her spell released in a moment. On the podium, Rune was patting his pocket. Brand sighed and said, "Like fucking clockwork."

Rune recovered from the lost speech. Everyone clapped and was happy. Quinn pretended to be happy along with them.

He'd told himself to be quiet before he knew more. Now Quinn knew. If he raised the alarm, everyone on this lawn would die. It was an absolute certainty—a giant scissor blade severing all future timelines.

So he kept his mouth shut and enjoyed the last night of his

life. Because no matter what Lady Time promised, there weren't many other ways he could interpret the utter darkness he saw in his own personal future.

"Are you sure you're alright?" Max hissed for the third time.

Quinn didn't need to answer because the limo took a tight left, and the kids all ended up slapped together like firewood.

Diana and Corinne were on one side of the comfortable bench seats, and Queenie's head poked above the half-lowered front seat partition. Quinn sat with Layne, Anna, and Max. Corbie was nodding off in Layne's lap.

Quinn wished Max would stop asking, because now Anna was looking at Quinn, and Anna was a whole other level of suspicious. Quinn never underestimated her.

"By the River," Diana said, slapping her phone down against the seat. "Another decorator quit. *By text.*"

"It can't be Brand's fault this time," Layne said, immediately taking his side.

"I'm not sure I would wager money on that," Diana said. "She came to me this afternoon because, and I quote, 'Lord Brandon was upset there was no knife block in the design plans.'"

"We already have a knife block," Anna said.

"Not in the basement family room," Diana amended. Her gaze sharpened a second before the car turned again, and then they bumped over the heavily cracked, tarred road leading up to the front of Sun Estate.

Quinn spotted a line of guards along the road, both Rune's small Arcanum contingent and those loaned from the Tower's security force. Quinn would need to be careful sneaking past them tonight. Midnight was not far off.

"What?" Anna said, looking hard at him.

"What what?" Quinn said back at her.

She just stared. Anna didn't waste words. She'd asked a question, and now waited for her answer.

"Just tired," Quinn said. He faked a yawn and patted his mouth. "I'll put Corbie to bed and maybe we can make some popcorn and hot chocolate."

Against Layne's chest, Corbie mumbled the word *acorns*, and went back to sleep.

When the car stopped, Layne handed Corbie to Quinn with a word of thanks, and Quinn carried Corbie into the mansion while everyone else split off to the kitchen.

There were guards inside the house, too, but they didn't stop Quinn as he busied himself with putting Corbie into his bed. He paused only long enough to whisper some words of advice to the little man. The six-year-old might not have that growling intensity to his future like Anna did, but, oh, what a life Corbitant had ahead of him. He kissed the boy on the forehead, said the word *brother*, and hurried off to his room.

Max would come looking for him soon, so he wasted no time.

The first thing he did was write a letter to Addam. Then he cried. Then he wiped his eyes and began to throw a few items into a backpack—mostly underwear and a second pair of shoes. He thought about writing letters to everyone else, then got confused because he couldn't remember if this was the lifetime where he had a pen pal named Reno in Helsinki, and he'd want to say goodbye to Reno too.

Running out of time, he turned his attention to thwarting Anna and Max, who almost certainly would try to come after him. The best idea he had was to hide their shoes—so he hauled everything from their bedrooms and dumped them into a linen closet, then snuck downstairs and hid all the shoes in the main hall.

Then it was a quarter to midnight, and he heard voices calling his name from the ballroom. Someone turned on a television.

Quinn snuck out a side door that wouldn't be watched. On the threshold, he closed his eyes briefly and whispered, "I love you all. I have lived *lifetimes* with you in my head. They were good lives."

From inside the mansion, he felt… a reply. That was the best way to describe it. Like something powerful and vast raising its head to blink at him—not unlike a metaphor for Rune and Anna's powers.

"Shit," Quinn said.

He hot-footed it through a path where he wouldn't be observed. As Quinn hurried, he felt timelines fray and snap and then weave together into a wholly new picture. He thought maybe he'd tempted fate a little too much.

Then he saw Max leaning against the old gate of a split-rail fence. His best friend wore his nice training boots—which Quinn had forgotten to steal. Corbie sometimes swiped them so he could wade into the pond after tadpoles.

"Let me guess," Quinn sighed. "Anna had a gut instinct and told you to look for me."

"You need to tell me what's going on," Max said in a very serious voice. His eyes were bloodshot and pinched—the way eyes got when Atlanteans used a migraine-inducing sober cantrip.

"There's no time. I need you to go back inside. I need you to trust me. Nothing has ever been more important than this, Max."

"I understand," Max said. Then he pulled out his phone and began tapping on it.

"What are you doing?" Quinn said.

"Texting Addam to tell him you're hiding prophecies again."

"You wouldn't dare!"

"I dare. I'm daring. I'm halfway through texting my dare."

Without thinking, Quinn slapped the phone out of Max's hand. It arced into the brush and made a cracking sound, like it had struck rock.

"They die tonight if you call," Quinn said before Max could shout.

Max's jaw sagged.

"I know who Lady Jade is," Quinn said. "She's Time."

"Time for what?"

"Time. The Hourglass Throne. The Hourglass Throne is back. If I don't go to her, she will kill Addam. She will kill Rune and Brand and everyone. If I don't go to her, she'll strike now, and it will end. It will all end. I swear to you on my life it's true, I've Seen it. I swear to you on *Addam's* life it's true."

"This is fucked," Max said. "This is fucked up, Quinn! You can't—"

"She said she'll treat me like a noble prisoner. There are rules about that. I'll be safe, if I do what she says."

Max stared at him as if he spotted the uncertainty.

"Please," Quinn said.

Max nodded slowly. "I'm coming with you."

Quinn was a half-second away from protesting until, suddenly, he didn't. He couldn't. Because Max was right. He did come with Quinn.

"We need to keep walking," Quinn said in resignation. "I'm supposed to meet them at midnight."

CHAPTER TWO

Quinn

They buried Max's sigil and cracked mobile phone on the edge of Sun Estate. Max tried to argue for hiding or swallowing his cameo sigil, but Quinn was insistent. Whatever they had on them would be taken, and Max would be miserable about losing his cameo for years and years and years.

(He could see Max lamenting about it to everyone except Quinn, because Quinn didn't see himself in any of those scenes. Not even the time when the birthday hat cones were on everyone's heads.)

"What is wrong with you?" Max hissed as they crossed an empty late-night road. The nearby park sat like a black pond ahead, lit only sparsely by pools of streetlamp light. "What is that look on your face? What aren't you telling me?"

"A lot, I suppose," Quinn said honestly. "Just promise me you'll pay attention?"

"Does something about being kidnapped make you think I'm going to doze off and daydream?"

Quinn didn't answer. He heard whitewater rapids in his head. Ahead of them, in the park's darkness, he saw the writhing energy of a critical moment. A juncture. In a minute, they'd be able to see the streetlamps glinting off the side mirrors of the parked cars.

There was no time for subtlety. Quinn called on his powers

and *pushed*, sending his mind's eye racing ahead by tens of minutes in a blink. There. There and there. There. He spotted the places where fate eddied into unreliable whorls—troubling decision points to be avoided at all costs.

"Max, listen," Quinn whispered urgently. "Watch out for the one with the paint on his clothes. He's not nice. Vadik is a snake—or he's pretending to be a snake, but he still has a lot of poison in him, just like a snake would. And—"

Oh. Oh, this last one hurt.

"And when I ask the guards to hold you, just trust me. It will keep you safe." Quinn swallowed and ducked his eyes to avoid Max's stare.

"Vadik?" Max repeated. "Isn't that the scion who Rune doesn't like?"

Quinn blinked. It was. *Son of a—!* Comprehension caught up with prophecy. "He tricked me," Quinn said angrily. "He was there when Rune and Anna were attacked. He did something to trick me!"

"Okay, but why are you speaking all prophet-like," Max said. "Why are you telling me all this now?"

At that moment, the headlights of the parked cars flicked on. The engines coughed alive.

"Even Rune gives better hand signals when shit is about to go down," Max accused.

Quinn put aside his own indignation and *pushed* harder. His voice shook and a crooked line of warmth on his upper lip told him he had a nosebleed. "Listen to me, Max. Find the Fiddle. The Fool is fractured—be kind. Trust Juror. And oh my *gods*, Anna, what the heck are you doing? What are you looking at? What is that?"

Quinn's gaze darted back and forth, excited. He knew Max was about to panic, but his friend had enough self-control not to grab Quinn's shoulders or shake him out of the trance. Every word that left Quinn's lips was a Truth—a road paved in asphalt, not dirt. Max needed to hear as much as Quinn could say in whatever time was left. His own moment of darkness was so close. It was so close.

And then—there, on the far horizon of his prophecy. He *pushed* toward it. The roar in his head grew louder.

"Find the equipment and expose her ruse. That knowledge is the weapon Rune needs. I—you can find it—where where where? Endless bizarre hallways, so many hallways."

His magic faded. Random, dying flickers of power snagged on his surroundings, like a broken fingernail scraped along wool. *The girl falls here and scratches her shin. A man files bankruptcy papers from his phone. A woman laughs and drops to her knees, pulling her engagement ring out of her pocket just after her girlfriend offers one of her own.* Quinn let his gaze stay on that—that pulsating bit of happiness.

"Quinn, they're coming," Max said urgently.

"I know," Quinn said. "Max, remember everything I'm saying. You'll be alright if you remember."

"But…" Max grabbed Quinn's sleeve and tugged, surprising his friend into a direct stare. "Why won't you remember? Does this all make *you* okay, too?"

So good, Quinn thought again. *He is getting so good at asking questions.*

"I will be okay if you're okay," Quinn said, a perfectly true lie.

And then magic rushed over them. Quinn's eyes rolled up into blackness, and his knees buckled under him. Max grabbed him—or grabbed onto Quinn because Max was moaning and falling too.

He heard a man say, clearly, "Put them in the trunk."

Quinn slept.

Quinn woke up.

He was lying horizontal, supported by thin air and enemy magic. *Telekinesis.* He was being carted down a hall with Telekinesis, which made anger flare in his brain because only

Addam had ever lifted him with Telekinesis before.

"—down!" Max was shouting, who was already awake and more than a little angry himself.

The magic encasing Quinn vanished. He collapsed to a dirty tiled floor, staring up at a ballroom ceiling that may have been lovely except for the grime and spider webs. They were so old and thick that they twisted overhead like used bedsheets.

There were two guards with them. One wore an urban camo jacket splattered with dark gray paint, and had red sideburns and freckles.

"Happy?" he said with a sneer, and reached out a hand as if to help Max up.

Quinn may have hit the ground harder than he expected because he didn't have enough air in his lungs to warn Max.

Maybe Max remembered the warning, maybe he didn't, but he slapped the man's hand away and climbed to his feet. But before he found his balance, the guard shoved Max against a wall. Max hit the hard marble panels with a crack. His scrabbling hands cleared patches in the dust.

Quinn found his second wind.

"You will not do that again," he gasped, and got up.

"Will I not?" the man mocked.

Time. Time was running out. So little time to make sure Max would be safe.

Quinn called on his power again, but it felt sluggish and slow to respond. So he pushed and he pushed and he pushed, until the swirling motes of prophecy formed a ragged intuition to the best path forward.

"Your jacket is splattered with paint from when you knocked someone off a ladder while they were doing repairs," Quinn said, and his voice trembled with ability. "I see you. You are a mean and sullen bully. I can hear you brag about the bees and flies and spiders on the ground in front of you—when you were young, you would pull off their wings and legs, waiting for them to die. I'm sorry no one helped you when there was time to make a difference. But you're old enough to know right from wrong. If you keep doing the wrong thing, I will tell you when you die. I will tell you how you are killed. It's not as far off as—"

"*Enough,*" a voice cracked across the ballroom.

In a nearby archway stood a man covered—head to feet—in scaly green leather.

Quinn stared at this new man for a full five seconds and let his gift play through the future until seeing a moment when the man's identity was revealed. He said, "That won't fool Rune for long, Vadik Amberson."

If Vadik had a reaction, it was hidden beneath the mask. His impassive face turned to Quinn. "I look forward to him realizing what this mask means."

"You shouldn't," Quinn whispered. "It's all darkness after that."

"Watch them," Vadik barked at a guard—but not the one with paint on his jacket, who looked thoroughly freaked out. "Lady Time will see them in a moment."

He swept out of the room, snapping his finger at Paint Man to follow him. That was the only apparent exit from the room. There was one other ornate archway, but it ended in a cavern wall's natural, craggy face.

Max and Quinn went to it since it was far enough away from the remaining guard to whisper. "What is this?" Max hissed, touching the bare rock. "Where are we? Is this the Warrens?"

"I think so," Quinn said. He scratched his lip. "I think. No, I'm sure. There's a name for this place, but I don't see it yet. It resists me. There's..." He searched for the right words. "Interference."

"Magical interference?" Max said.

"The opposite. There's so *little* magic here. I can't understand it. It's not like a normal translocation." He shook away the thoughts, which were a distraction eating away what little time he had left. He could feel the inexorable pull to the nearby Arcana—she was close, and almost made the walls between them burn with energy.

He grabbed both of Max's hands and squeezed. "Listen to me," Quinn said. "I know you're scared, but you must be careful around Lady Time. She is strong. She is so, so strong."

"So was Rurik, but Brand shot him in the head. Can I shoot her in the head?"

Maybe Max was a little more angry than scared.

But then, just like that, they were out of time. Vadik returned to the archway alone. His scaled mask regarded them quietly. He dismissed the remaining guard with a jerk of his head and crooked his finger at Quinn and Max. Max had enough sense to grab the backpack that Quinn nearly forgot.

They followed him down a dirty but somewhat regal hallway toward a set of ornate wooden double doors. Every window they passed showed only a craggy rock face—no yard or anything like that. What furniture they saw was twentieth century, but the surfaces were stained and patchy with disuse.

Quinn darted a look at Max to ensure his friend was paying attention. Every detail would help him later. Quinn only wished he had more time to look ahead and prepare himself. But his own future lay behind the doors ahead. Every path in front of Quinn ended in that room.

Vadik opened both doors at once, and stepped aside to let the boys pass. A thin tapestry covered the mouth of the room in front of them, turning the area in front of the doorway into an antechamber. The edges of it were covered in the silky furrows of a moth infestation.

From the other side of the tapestry, Quinn heard a door slam shut—or maybe open, he thought, because a stale breeze caused the tapestry to ruffle. Then Lady Time said, "Is the next group ready?"

A man responded—quickly, before she barely finished speaking, "The prisoners have arrived, my lady."

The tapestry parted—magically—sending a cough of dust into Quinn's face. He spotted Lady Time on the other side of a large, cozy, clean room, her hand paused mid-wave.

"Little prophet," she crooned. "So kind of you to spare us any dramatics, although I didn't expect you to invite witnesses."

Quinn snuck a quick look at Max—who seemed fascinated by the advanced age of the woman in front of him. Hoping he'd stay quiet and not antagonize the Arcana, Quinn licked his dry lips and took a step forward.

"You'll treat us both like formal prisoners?" Quinn said. *"Both* of us?"

Lady Time stared at him, one eyebrow quivering in a half-raise, then waved her hand dismissively. She shifted her eyes to a man in a simple cotton cloak.

He was old—a normal old, maybe a decade shy of the age that most Atlanteans rejuvenated. Or... *oh*. No. Quinn was not seeing the truth. There was a haze about that man that signaled deception. His true nature was hidden or glamored.

Lady Time said, "The elixir, Cornelius?"

The fussy, thin person angled a hand toward the center of the room. The chamber was a mix of old, ruined luxury; deep cleaning; and cheap new department store merchandise. A long, folding banquet table sat under the weight of plated food—most untouched, with some dishes already showing congealed butter and fats.

Quinn wasn't sure what this Cornelius was pointing toward.

"You," Lady Time said, and stared at Max. "That look of naked calculation on your face is exhausting. You stand in the presence of an Arcana and three principalities. You'll want to save your energy for another pointless display of resistance."

Quinn thought to himself, *Three?*, but too much was going on to focus on any one detail. Lady Time was sweeping across the chamber to the most throne-like chair available to her—a giant, padded beast that fanned her head in red velvet. She sat and crossed one thin leg over the other. Her dress, simple but oversized, hung below bare feet.

"Atlanteans have regressed," Lady Time said. Beside her, on

a tall round table, was a collection of items that looked like sigils. She ran her fingers through the rings and pendants. "I don't quite understand it yet. What has changed? Why are you so much smaller? Are your magics that much less? Has Atlantis grown afraid—or shy of exerting our true authority under the suffocating, sweating bulk of humanity? The human war was an atrocity. I'm not sure who or what stayed our hand, but the capital of every country should rightfully be a charred crater—and we should have had our pick of every inch of land, of every mountain, every forest and glade, every sea and river. We stare down at the food chain—the food chain does not stare down on us."

She flicked the lines of sigils into disarray. "Even these are weak and flavorless. Like trinkets. It's as pathetic as the *shared* magics—the modern trend to binding sigils to families. When I finally find a sigil style I like best, I'll need to slaughter the house that owns them down to the last child to claim them."

"Why are you doing this?" Max asked.

"Because this is the nature of power," she said. "Your friend with the messy hair understands. His power makes my eyes ache. An awesome gift, clairvoyance. Always feared. Always mistrusted. A recipe for madness and misdirection in weaker hands. Did you know, little prophet, that there was once a type of far-sight that could only be used during earthquakes? Prophecies were interpreted by the pattern of falling rune stones, but the rune stones may only be upset by the movement of the world's tectonic plates—as if the entire planet itself was throwing ivory dice into the gaming bowl. In a very real sense, prophecy was almost as feared as time magic. Though fear, of course, breeds its own form of respect and reverence. Your forebears were *revered* little prophet. Piled in jewels and anointed in oils, in my day."

"What *day?*" Max asked. "So you came from another time? Can you go back there? If we're all so weak and flavorless, why not return?"

"Why would I return?" she said. "I am adept at the most

powerful branch of magic ever devised. My own peers were loath to let us practice it. But I suspect the rulers of these modern days will be much less able to resist my more… persuasive arguments."

"The Arcanum will never allow it," Max said. "Never. I know enough about time magic to know there's a reason the Hourglass Throne doesn't exist anymore."

"You know nothing," she laughed. The sound managed to be both dry and phlegmatic at the same time.

"No, I get it," Max said. "Your time had powerful people, big magic, and lots of soliloquies. But things are different now."

MAX, Quinn thought, wishing not for the first time he knew how to mentally kick someone in the head like Rune and Brand did with each other.

Lady Time uncrossed her legs and leaned back on her makeshift throne. "Would you like me to share a secret with you? Listen closely. People today have an obscured view of *why* the Hourglass Throne fell. It's quite simple. Our most unforgivable act was being able to do what no other court could.

"We used time magic to know the best possible outcome in advance, and thus ensured the timeline that served us best. We made the perfect investments. We always knew the right thing to say. We knew the outcome of every fight before we waged it. We knew the perfect genetic combinations to have the most talented, powerful heirs. I am their crowning achievement— the result of hundreds upon hundreds of careful decisions based on foreknowledge. But our edge was not to be tolerated by the rest of the courts. They said it was about the damage to the timeline, but it's all lies. They were arrogant, weaker beasts, and our advantage was not to be borne. Much like our little prophet here—we were taken off the game board."

Quinn's entire life narrowed to the single moment before them. He heard her words a heartbeat before she would actually say them.

Lady Time pointed to a plain brass goblet on the table. "Drink that, child."

Quinn took a slow breath and said, "I think you should hold Max now."

A lot of things happened quickly. A red-haired young woman—who'd blended so seamlessly into the backdrop of a wall hanging that it must have been magical—jumped forward and pulled Max's arms behind him.

And Max went effing bananas.

It was a chaos of thrashing and shouts until Quinn saw Max's fingernails grow to extra-sharp length—one of his fae traits. Only then did Quinn lunge toward Max, finding the perfect moment to grab Max's face in both hands.

"You listen to me, Matthias Saint John!" Quinn shouted desperately. "You tell Addam I love him! You tell Addam I—" Quinn felt his heart shatter, all splintered bits of pulp and rib cage. "You tell them all I love them—Christian, Diana, my mom, Ella—you tell them all. And you tell… you tell my real family…"

Max went still. He whispered, "Quinn, don't. Don't."

Quinn's voice dropped to a whisper, too. "And you tell my *real* family that I spent my entire life fighting my way toward them." He spread his thumbs out so he was cupping his friend's face. "Do you know how many futures I saw? How many decisions I had to make? Just to get closer and closer to my best friend in my best future? I am so lucky I had that, even for a little while."

Quinn stepped away from Max and grabbed the goblet. The liquid inside was warm, heating the brass.

He drank it in one long, breathless sip while Max *screamed* behind him.

The potion tasted like wintergreen and latte foam. It hit his stomach, rebelled, and launched back up his throat into his mouth, tunneling through his sinus cavity like it was moving right toward his brain.

Everything turned a blinding, sun-washed white.

He hit the ground before the goblet did.

CHAPTER THREE
Max

Max's anger vanished, replaced by a still and icy numbness.

He would find Addam, and tell him about Quinn, and the two of them would burn Lady Time's world to the ground. They would find and hurt everyone in this room. They would not rest until it was ashes and rubble.

The arms around him were released.

Lady Time might have said something? He wasn't sure.

He stumbled over to Quinn, and either fell or dropped to his knees. The young man's face was pale, and he wasn't moving, and part of Max's soul was dying.

"Don't," he whispered. He put his face down to Quinn's lips, eyes closed tight, trying to feel Quinn's breath against his own cheek. "Don't leave me, Quinn. Don't leave me don't leave me don't leave me." His tears fell on his best friend's bloodless cheek.

He screamed for Addam in his head. He screamed for Rune, and Brand, and anything in the universe that might hear him and help.

Then Quinn's eyes opened.

Their faces were so close that Max felt the brush of an eyelash. He jerked back and saw a look of puzzled bleariness on Quinn's face.

"Are you dead?" Quinn said. "Are you dead too? Don't be dead Max!"

Max raised his hot gaze to Lady Time, who smirked at them both from the other side of the banquet table. She'd got up from her throne at some point and moved closer.

"What have you done?" he growled.

"I took the prophet off the game board. Just as I said. Rise, Quinn. *Rise now.*"

Quinn sucked in a breath. Max grabbed Quinn under the armpits and tried to lever him upright—not because the witch had asked, but just to make sure Quinn *could* stand, just to make sure he was *alright.*

"Now," Lady Time said. "Walk around the table. Come to me."

Quinn didn't seem to have any better idea what was going on. He frowned at Max, but gave an *I'm-okay* shoulder shrug and moved toward the table. It was in front of him, so he'd need to go around it.

Quinn looked left. Then he looked right. Then he went from pale to ashen and looked at *everything*—up, down, the doors, the people, *everything*. With a sound of distress, he backpedaled from the table and threw himself at Max.

"What?" Max whispered urgently as Quinn clung to him and shivered. His alarm returned. "What did you do to him!"

"Jerica will show you to your rooms," Lady Time said. "If you continue to act like a noble prisoner, you will be treated as a noble prisoner. You may not attempt to communicate with anyone outside the Eidolon, nor escape it, nor undermine my rule. Should you do otherwise, the consequences will be profound. And permanent. Do you understand?"

"No!" Max shouted. "Who is Jerica? What is the Eidolon? *And what did you do to Quinn?*"

But the Arcana had said what she wanted to say. Brushing aside his questions with a thin, viperous smile, she exited through a door at the side of the room. Everyone but the red-haired woman followed her.

The woman was short and curvy, with dark skin and bushy,

dyed-crimson hair that looked like it had been doused in 1980s-strength fluorocarbons. She had guarda zip-ties as bracelets and wore a red halter top over a red bell-bottomed pantsuit.

"Well, he's a Saint Nicholas, alright," she said in a quiet, deep voice, leaning forward at an angle to stare into Quinn's bleary burgundy eyes. She switched her attention to Max. "I'm Jerica. He'll be okay."

"It's like flying," Quinn said against Max's chest. "It's like when I fly to the top of mountains with Addam—when I fly so fast-fast-fast I can't see anything. I can't see anything, Max."

"How is this okay?" Max demanded to the stranger.

"Look," she said. "Has his prophecy been whacked the last few days? Did he stop seeing *himself* in his futures? That's usually a sign the potion is going to work. It sort of makes your brain hurt to figure out why it would work that way, but it's true. That's what Cornelius says, at least."

"What are you talking about?" Max demanded in frustration. "He's been fine! What is—" His mouth clicked shut as he caught the expression on Quinn's face.

"Maybe a little?" Quinn whispered.

"Oh my gods," Max hissed. "If Addam doesn't finally get mad at you I will lose my *shit*."

Quinn seemed to decide that clinging to an angry Max wasn't a good idea. He backed up and began staring around him. His attention snagged on every mundane detail like a wobbly-legged fawn wondering where the godsdamn womb had gone.

Then Quinn smiled.

"But flying can be fun sometimes," he said to no one in particular.

"Can anyone tell me what's happening?" Max begged.

"Not here," Jerica said. *"Listen to me.* I… know Rune. And Brand. I like them—we trade information on occasion. I'll do what I can to help you, but I can't do anything against *her.* You are only as safe as her mood. We really, really should be anywhere but here."

"But what was in that potion?" Max asked.

"It tasted like mint," Quinn said excitedly and unhelpfully. "But toothpaste mint, not after-dinner-candy mint. And I can't see the future anymore. Any future. I don't even know what door we should go through!"

The expression on Jerica's face, combined with Quinn's apparent daze, convinced him that moving was prudent. He grabbed Quinn's sleeve and yanked him toward the same door they'd entered, following Jerica.

As they made their way down the mansion-like hallway, Max said, "You know Rune and Brand?"

Jerica shrug-nodded, and turned right down a side corridor. It looked more abandoned than anything else Max had seen yet; Jerica began poking at large spider webs with a chair leg she kept looped in her belt.

"But you know *her*, too? The woman who calls herself Lady Time?"

"She's Lady Time alright," Jerica said.

"Did…" Max swallowed. "Is everyone OK? Are Rune and Brand okay?"

"I made sure they were," Quinn said dreamily. "I told you. That's why I was quiet as a mouse at the gala, so she wouldn't hurt them."

"Was she being serious?" Max asked, still looking at Jerica. "When she said she'd slaughter an entire house to get sigils? Could she actually do that—like she did at the rejuvenation center? That was all her?"

"All her," Jerica murmured. "Let's find you a room so you can stay out of her way."

"But…" Max trailed off again. He'd been looking for signs of where they might be, but there were no windows or open doorways. No convenient mail left on an end table with a clearly marked address. *Because most evil lairs have a mailing address, you idiot.*

"We're underground?" he confirmed.

"Yes. Do not try to run—it's dangerous outside the Eidolon."

"And this building is called the Eidolon?"

"Oh, left!" Quinn shouted as they approached an intersection. "Can we go left? I don't know what's left *or* right, Max!"

Then Quinn made a happy sound. There was a moldering tapestry strung along a wall that, at second glance, turned out to be drapes. Quinn ran over, grabbed them, and yanked so hard they made a brittle ripping sound and collapsed to the carpet in a heap.

On the other side was a massive picture window. It faced a rock wall covered with wormlike creatures the size of ship harpoons. They had burrowed antlike trails into the stone. They also appeared to be messy cannibals, judging from the bits of gore and fleshy pulp smeared along the glass.

Quinn sucked in a horrified breath. "That was not a good choice." He brightened immediately. "I just made my first bad choice!"

"Not even this hour, Quinn," Max said.

Jerica sighed and said, "Just stay away from the bloodworms. Or bring fire to scare them off. And actually, we really do need to go left. Come on, he'll be fine. Cornelius always spikes his potions with stimulants."

They turned and finally passed an open doorway. Thick cords snaked in—or out?—of it, and Max recognized the rumble of a generator before he spotted it. The smell of gas fumes faded as they continued down the hallway.

Since Jerica wasn't precisely unhelpful, Max went ahead and said, "So we're in the Warrens?"

"Sort of. But close to the Lowlands. You heard me when I told you not to go outside?"

Max stopped walking so quickly that Quinn slammed into his back. He said, "We're near the Lowlands?"

"Did those look like average earthworms?"

Max swallowed and started walking again. The Lowlands were far, far below the bedrock. Not even Rune or Brand had ever gone there. It was a massive, uncharted subterranean land. There were no human records of a cave system on the island; the first mentions of the Lowlands began right about the same time the Westlands started to grow. It was spoiled with crazy, wild magic. A dangerous part of a dangerous island of a dangerous people.

"Rune is going to kill us," he whispered.

"Addam will understand," Quinn said with misplaced confidence.

"When we stole a boat, they made us go to school. Now we let ourselves get kidnapped to the Lowlands. We'll have doctorates before they let us out of our room."

"In there," Jerica said. "We can talk more outside."

"You said not to go outside," Max told her.

"Outside the safe areas. Well, safer areas."

"And in *where?*" Max demanded. He pointed at an opening in the wall. "In that? Is that a dumbwaiter?"

"The main stairs got crushed in the translocation, and I'd rather not take us through *her* wing. There's a knotted rope inside—it'll get us to the first floor. I'll send a cantrip ahead." She twirled a finger in the air and whispered a few words. A tiny ball of bright white light zipped ahead of them.

Max had been practicing his own magic. He'd gotten better since Rune began teaching him sigil use, but he still struggled with the basics. He tried to manifest his own light cantrip… and failed. Even worse than usual. It was like trying to suck a sip of water through a mouthful of sand.

He exchanged a quick look with Quinn, who seemed to be having his own trouble. His friend was staring in curiosity at his snapping fingers, looking for the spark of magic.

"I don't get it," Max murmured. "We can't be in a null zone. You just used magic."

"It's a long story," Jerica said. She knocked on the frame of the dumbwaiter. "Remember when I said we could talk more outside?"

Max wished he'd been quicker on putting the pieces together.

Three principalities.

He'd never even seen Jerica until she revealed herself.

Allowed in Lady Jade's—Lady Time's—presence.

"You're a principality," he said.

"You're Fiddler Blue," Quinn added, which made Jerica curtsy with an eye roll.

Max glared at Quinn, who seemed surprised he wasn't glaring at Jerica. Max was beginning to understand why Rune sometimes got a thick pulse on his forehead when Quinn was being particularly evasive with his prophecies.

Shelving his irritation, he swung his legs over the lip of the dumbwaiter shaft. There was a thick, knotted hemp rope hanging there. Max tugged on it, and felt the loose give of several stories of length above him. But Jerica's light cantrip was bright enough below to show less than a twenty-foot drop.

He braced his feet against the side of the chute and descended, the way Brand had taught him to keep from tearing up his palms. He looked up and saw Quinn's jeans sticking out of the dumbwaiter above him in an awkward V, sighed, got his footing, and reached up to grab Quinn when Quinn eventually slipped and began to fall down the shaft.

"Normally I'd levitate," his friend said defensively as they detangled arms and legs. Then Quinn noticed the exit from the dumbwaiter shaft and lost interest in anything but what was on the other side. He wiggled past Max and climbed out.

"We go in here?" Max said up the shaft to where Jerica was swinging down.

"It's safe," she said. "Wait for me in the kitchen. *Do not open the refrigerator!*"

Max swore and stuck his head out of the dumbwaiter just as Quinn reached for the fridge handle. He'd somehow found the time to yank open two drawers and an empty cupboard along the way.

"Don't worry, I heard her," Quinn said over his shoulder. "I'll check it first to make sure it's safe. I don't know what's in it!"

"That is literally the point," Max shouted back while clambering through the opening. The lintel was dry-rotted and crumbled under his hands. He heard the thud of Jerica landing behind him.

"It's the stench," she said. "Gods know what was in there before the translocation. It's like if a bad smell had an asshole."

The kitchen was easily identified as a mansion-sized kitchen, despite the fact that most appliances and fixtures had been long since stripped and removed. Quinn had, thankfully, abandoned the dented and dirty fridge in favor of standing by the dry sink—and the window over it. Orange light flickered through the grimy glass.

"I think it's a cave," Quinn said.

"Remember the worms?" Max demanded.

"I didn't like that. They were eating each other."

Jerica—*Fiddler Blue?*—climbed into the kitchen and brushed off the lap of her reddish-magenta bell bottoms. "Actually, that's one of the safe areas. I warded it myself. We can catch our breath outside and chat."

Max put his hands on Quinn's shoulders and nudge-shoved his friend out a simple back door with a tattered daffodil-yellow fringed curtain.

"Holy crap," Max whispered as the guttering light of real torches revealed a massive cavern with its ceiling lost to shadow.

The space was a courtyard in only the barest of senses—an enclosed space surrounded by larger buildings. Only the space was deep underground, and the buildings were surreal. It looked as if two or three mansions had been jammed together at different angles. One attic had been crushed entirely; another mansion rested off-kilter at a forty-five-degree angle. The mansion they'd just emerged from was one of the least damaged. The outside wall was covered with colorful paintball-gun graffiti.

"So the Eidolon is three big-ass buildings," Max concluded.

"These are just Lady Time's fuck-ups," Jerica said. "Came from Rhode Island after the storm."

"This is her fuck-up? She caused this?" Max said.

"No—it's just a saying. Every bad translocation is like its own city block. Its own fuck-up. These mansions came from Rhode Island in America. The tsunamis that took out Newport? During the Atlantean War? These buildings came from there. But they were still mansions with a fucked up past, so at least there's a thread of magic to pull on." She said the last part as a grumble.

Max knew there was a lot of information in what the young woman—old woman? Ancient woman? *Who knew with principalities?*—said. He asked, "So the Eidolon is from Rhode Island?"

"The Eidolon is from everywhere. Ski chalets, a housing project, about twenty McMansion fuck-ups—it just goes on and on. We haven't even found all of it yet."

"But..." Curiosity was eating through Quinn's high. "Ski chalets? That can't be right. Who would translocate ski chalets? You could build a hundred for the cost of moving just one."

"There are about fifty of them, stacked on top of each other like honeycomb. The village was about to get flooded out—climate change. I guess they got a good deal."

"But who are *they?*" Max asked. "Did the Hex Throne run these translocations too?"

Jerica did one of her shrug-nod-headshake things that answered precisely nothing, in either the affirmative or negative. "Either way, no one ever really moved in until Lady Time breached an opening and set up her base."

She clapped her hands together. "Okay. I put some sound buffers into the protection wards around the courtyard. I doubt anyone else here except Vadik and Cornelius could spy on us—but *she* could if she wanted. Remember that."

"How strong is she? We've faced other Arcana before, you know."

Jerica actually laughed. "*You know?* Of course I know. Rune is a freaking bull in the Arcanum gift shop. But Lady Time… she's not like us. She's not from this era. You can't face her. I can't face her. I'm not sure the entire Arcanum could easily face her. I'm not sure how she got as strong as she did—but she did."

Max stared around them, taking in the enormous cathedral of rock above their head. He'd be a lot more lost if he didn't have a Quinn in his life.

But he did have a Quinn, and the sixteen-year-old prophet had already spoken:

Find the equipment and expose her ruse. That knowledge is the weapon Rune needs.

"She didn't order us to stay in our rooms, right?" Max asked.

Jerica sighed. "No. Common sense is ordering you to stay in your rooms. At least for tonight. I'll…" She growled, put her hands in her stiff hairstyle and scratched. "I need to think about what I can do."

"But you said you're friends with Rune and Brand."

"I said I *know* them. And we're friendlyish."

"I don't understand," Max said honestly. "Rune has mentioned you. You're one of his contacts when he's gathering data for cases, right? He trusts you. Why would you join up with someone like this?"

Jerica didn't answer right away. She studied Quinn instead, who was bouncing from shiny thing to shiny thing—while keeping a wary eye out for giant worms. She murmured, "I'll bring him to Cornelius tomorrow, so you can learn more about what's happened to him."

"Quinn told me to find the fiddle," Max pressed. "That means he trusts you—"

"*Prophecy* trusts her," Quinn said while gently kicking an

old, standing ashtray made out of crystal and gold plating.

"—so you can't be all evil," Max insisted.

"This isn't your first rodeo, kid," Jerica said. "You know as well as I do that shit happens, and it has nothing to do with good or evil. You think she's bad? Her?" Jerica pointed back at the mansion. "Rune opened the door for her return—him and the Hanged Man, damn his eyes. Is Rune evil?"

"Rune… what? *What?*" Max demanded. "When did he do that?"

"When doesn't matter. It never does with time magic."

"But… So she's been here—on the island—for just a few months? And you're all just standing here blindly following her? Did you see photos from the rejuvenation clinic? She massacred those people. They didn't have sigils or weapons. This is who you follow? Someone you met months ago?"

Jerica marched right up to Max and poked a finger toward his chest. "You. Do. Not. Get. It. Months? You think this started months ago? She's been in my head since I was *a child*. She spent her entire adult life in a hellscape, tunneling toward the probability of a single second. This isn't her *advance*, this is her *endgame*. You cannot stop her—you can only survive."

"It's okay, Max," Quinn said. He was squatting next to an overturned milk crate, which turned out to be nothing more than an overturned milk crate. "She doesn't get it either."

"Get what?" Jerica asked, a little peevishly.

Quinn smiled at her. "That this is my endgame, too."

CHAPTER FOUR
Max

Max could see Jerica shake off a shiver.

"Your brother Addam did a good job hiding you from the world," she said. "I think I know why Lady Time is so unsettled by you. But… the potion. It worked? Your gift is muted?"

"I don't need to know the future right now," Quinn said. "I've already lived it dozens and dozens of times. I just need to remember it. But maybe later? I'm getting really tired."

Jerica seized on the distraction to change the subject. "There's a room over there, past the patio. There should be clean linens inside—there's a deka assigned here every day. A work detail. You'll hear them banging about in a few hours, so draw your drapes if you want privacy."

"I want to talk to you," Max said, changing the subject right back where he wanted it. "This isn't the sort of thing where you can play both sides."

"This is exactly that sort of thing," Fiddler said. "The idea of sides is an Arcanum concept. It's how they divide us. And the sides are always about them and who they fight. It has nothing—nothing!—to do with the people who die. There are real people down here, Matthias Saint John. They're getting fed and housed, and they have a purpose. They're my concern, not the Iconsgison's reindeer games."

"Jerica?" Quinn said, but the next line was swallowed by a huge yawn. He blushed a little. "Sorry. I was going to say that

Rune only knocks down people who deserve it. I think you'll like us, if you give us a chance. But we can talk tomorrow, right? You don't need to pick any sides right now. No one does."

Max looked around and spotted the only patio in eyesight—though technically, it was the stuff that remains after a patio is hurtled through space and slammed against a cavern floor. But on the other side of the mounds of rubble was a set of French doors with clean white drapes hanging on clean glass.

"Stay inside. Get some rest. I'll be by again in about five hours. Okay?" Jerica said. "Please?"

"Five hours," Max agreed. Saying nothing else, he put an arm around his tired friend's shoulders and urged him toward the guest room.

Jerica hadn't lied. The room was prepared for guests, with linens that smelled like cheap, clean soap. Quinn took three giant steps toward a rollaway bed and collapsed face-first.

"Sleepy now," he sighed. "Are you going to pull the drapes for privacy?"

"Yes, Quinn. Privacy is at the top of the list. I'm even going to move this furniture in front of the door for extra privacy."

"That's sarcasm, right? Oh wow, sarcasm is going to be just as hard to spot as irony when I can't See what you're thinking."

Max finished pushing an empty bookshelf against the glass door. It wouldn't stop anyone, but it would make a lot of noise if someone tried to get through. The narrow, long room was once a sunroom or solarium, refitted with rollaway beds, a small milk crate of snacks and a single bottle of water, stacks of clean sheets, and a box of plain white candles. There was only one interior door, but it was boarded shut.

"Did you mean what you said outside?" Max asked when he was done. He sat down on the side of the second mattress. "About having a plan?"

"Sort of?"

"You're not just feeling arrogant because Lady Time flattered you? And said prophets should be anointed in oil? Like a salad?"

Since Quinn was Quinn, he laughed at the joke and pointed at Max as if to say *good one*. It was so hard to land snark on someone who preferred to cheer people on when they were being funny or brave.

Max unlaced his boots and pried them off. He'd sleep in his clothes, though. And also with the pocketknife he'd hidden in the hollow heel of his right boot. Brand wasn't raising a fool.

He had the uncomfortable sense that it was his job to direct the conversation. Quinn usually made emotional talk easy, because he always knew the right things to say to resolve it quickly and neatly. But things had happened tonight that Max needed to learn more about.

"Are you alright?" Max asked quietly. "It seemed scary. Losing your powers?"

Quinn slid his shoulders in another shrug.

"What's it like?" Max persisted.

"It's… awful. And it's a relief." He curled onto his side and stared at Max. "What people don't understand is that I live in my worst memories, too—not just the best. I live and I live and I *live* in the moments when I lost someone. The moments when I failed because I couldn't protect the people around me. It can mess with your mind. So this is like… a vacation."

"What if it's permanent?"

"Oh no," Quinn said. "No thank you. I don't like that option."

Max leaned forward with his elbows on his thighs, capturing Quinn's attention. "Did you come here thinking you were going to die?"

"I really *did!*" Quinn said, somehow evading Max's neatly laid plan to propel them into a potentially loud argument. Quinn went on, oblivious to Max's narrowed eyes. "But now that I know I didn't die? Things are starting to make a *lot* more sense. I know why we're here. We can help Rune. But maybe after some sleep. I really think I need to sleep now."

"I'll take first watch," Max sighed. "Get some rest."

Quinn started snoring halfway through thanking Max.

Max let Quinn sleep the entire time and tried to clear the sleepless night from his head with light meditation.

Someone had once told him deep meditation was a fae strength. Whether that was true or not, he didn't know, but he did find it easier to miss an evening's sleep than anyone else in his family. Except for Corbie, maybe, who Max suspected had an extra internal organ filled with high fructose corn syrup.

The morning staff arrived just like Jerica warned. They tried to be respectful, but their boots crunched on rock whenever they snuck too close to the windows to get a peek at the new guests.

The lights went out, too—sometime just before dawn. Max remembered where the box of candles was placed and managed to light a few without more than one shin bruise.

Eventually, Quinn began smacking his lips together and speaking nonsense words. On a normal night, this might be a good opportunity to whisper certain key phrases in his ear to fish for lottery numbers, even though Quinn insisted he couldn't see them and that was an obvious lie. But Quinn wasn't his usual self.

Was it permanent? Was this Quinn's new normal? The idea made Max's brain seize up. A prophetic Quinn *was* a normal Quinn.

"What time is it?" Quinn asked. Max almost missed it— Quinn had just been muttering about butterfly gardens a few seconds earlier.

"I don't know. There aren't any clocks. How are you feeling?"

"Hungry. But okay. Is Jerica back yet?" He leaned over the mattress's edge and fumbled for his backpack.

"Not yet. But there are people outside. Young, our age—

wearing lots of bright colors and ribbons. Too many colors to be one court's colors. Unless…"

Max paused and licked the corner of his lips distractedly. He only needed to shave once every couple of weeks, but he'd done a bad job last time. There was a single stubborn whisker poking back at his tongue.

"We need to learn more," he finally concluded.

"Oh!" Quinn exclaimed. He was holding a work boot from his backpack. Turning it around, he shook the boot gently, and a small electronic device slid from the inside, mounted to a wristband. "I didn't even realize I packed this. They didn't find it when they searched us."

"Is that the Magnus Slate?" Max said in astonishment.

"Yeah. No wireless signal. But look—it's six AM. And there's a light!" A flashlight beam sprang from the device as Quinn tapped it.

Gears started spinning so hard in Max's head that he nearly saw sparks. The Slate was designed for short-range school use, but it had a messaging function and emergency features. No signal meant no external contact—but could they get a signal? They wouldn't need to escape to help Rune; just find what he needed to know and call Anna's Slate.

He took it from Quinn, then turned the screen face up and swiped into the connectivity menu. He ran a quick search on signals to confirm there were none.

Gravel crunched outside the closed patio door. Max quickly slipped the Slate into his pocket as someone knocked. He called out an invitation and pushed the bookcase away from the threshold. The door cracked open slowly, making the candle flames stretch toward it in long, grasping threads.

"Good," Jerica said. "You found the candles. I forgot to mention those."

"The generator broke?" Max asked.

The principality edged further into the room. She'd swapped out her red jumpsuit for a shapeless yellow housecoat. Her red hair was teased into a beehive.

"We rotate it to different parts of the mansion," she said. "Most fuck-ups have planned brown-outs. Gas is expensive, and light cantrips are tricky down here. Anyway..." She scratched at her knuckles, a fidgety gesture. "My orders are clear. You're allowed to wander, but you can't do anything to escape, and you can't interfere."

"Interfere in what?" Quinn asked.

"Asking a question like that is interference," she said plainly.

And carefully. She was speaking very, very carefully. Max spotted that, and guessed she was trying to walk a narrow line. So he asked, just as carefully, "Where can we wander?"

"It depends," she said. "What do you want to see?"

One of the first things Brand had ever taught Max was that you needed a strategy to handle complex situations, and data informed tactics. So he needed *information*. He'd seen Lady Time's people and guards—but who were those teens dressed in bright colors? Who were those workers? How large was the Eidolon—who had built it, and what was its purpose? What was Lady Time *hiding* down here?

Knowledge informed tactics. Quinn said there was equipment down here that Rune needed to know about. Someone must know about it, or have seen or heard rumors.

Max wanted to go where people gathered and gossiped.

"Where does everyone hang out?" he asked. "I love crowds."

Jerica smiled at him. "Just our luck. It's raining topside. Follow me."

Shit got interesting after that.

That's what Max planned on writing in the mission report someday if Brand made him write one. *Shit got really interesting after that.*

Jerica had mentioned that there was more to the Eidolon than just the mansions. That became clear quickly. Jerica led them through a small crowd of workers raking up debris, into the ransacked kitchen, and down a short adjoining hallway. At the end of that corridor was the oversized front door, which was thrown open to what appeared to be a much, much smaller foyer of a different building entirely.

The next building was just as nice—lots of marble and real wood, and fancy columns that didn't have much to do with structural integrity.

"Is this what you called a McMansion?" Max guessed.

"Came from… North Carolina?" Jerica said. "Or maybe Connecticut. Some swanky housing development that failed during the big recession a decade ago in America."

"Not part of the Rhode Island mansions?"

"Not at all."

"And it landed just like that? Right up against the door of *this* mansion?" Max dragged his eyes away from the sight only long enough to catch Jerica's nod.

He knew a bit about translocations—they were a hobby of Rune's. This sort of precision was rare. Even in the Warrens, which were widely held to be the sort of mistake that could happen when you pulled too many buildings from outside New Atlantis into the city through a single act of translocation. There wasn't even a slope or step here—Max just walked out the mansion's front door, and into a smaller McMansion.

"Most of Lady Time's people have settled in the one good mansion," Jerica explained. "The others didn't make it here in one piece—wiring is shot. The McMansions are set aside for functions. Storage, cooking, laundry. We even have a house for live entertainment—no cable or wi-fi down here."

"No wi-fi anywhere?" Quinn asked, a little too obviously.

"Not that I've found, but I wouldn't ask people about it. I've already warned you about provoking her. Either you hear what I'm saying, or you don't—it's your choice."

The first McMansion looked like it was used for the storage of dry goods. They walked through a living room filled with mounds of toilet paper—half-finished rolls; unspooled rolls;

giant industrial rolls from department store restrooms. In the adjoining room were hundreds of containers of cleaning products—scuffed, old, new, cheap, brand-name. Everything looked stolen or donated, or both.

Max saw that and put it in the puzzle box. That was what Rune did. He made observations and threw them into a big mental box, and eventually, Rune's brain would cough and sputter and spit out a leap of insight.

To get to the next McMansion, they had to crawl through a bay window with missing glass. Old blankets had been placed on the lip to keep people from cutting themselves on shards or splinters.

That led to a smooth rock passage the length of a picnic table, and from there they crawled through a second-story window of another McMansion.

There were people in this one—mostly young, mostly wearing a motley of colors. Nearly all of them had ribbons in their hair, but all the ribbons were so different it was hard to spot a pattern or purpose.

This building had been designated for laundry. The air was redolent with steam and detergent, and while they'd gamely tried to protect the hard floors with plastic sheeting, water was everywhere. The smell of slowly rotting wood wasn't entirely unpleasant.

The wall of the master bedroom had been destroyed, leading to the master bedroom of another small mansion. The chemicals riding the air were replaced by the smell of chicken broth. They walked through the upstairs hallway, past a bathroom where a plywood board had been placed above a tub, and a woman with dreadlocks and ribbons sat cross-legged, dicing a small mound of green onions.

Jerica took them down an ornate staircase—something that'd be more at home in a palace, but scaled to a half-acre budget. "The No-TV TV House is that way. Follow the yellow line along that wall to head toward the supervisor's lunchroom. And if you backtracked to the attic, you'd see a passage to the

MZ. Short for Murder Zoo. The vegans named it—but it's where we keep poultry and rabbits for meat and eggs."

"Where are we going?" Quinn asked.

"You'll see."

They went to the basement of the cooking McMansion, where there was a low cement stairway covered by a metal swinging door, the sort of thing that usually led up to backyards in American houses. The cooking smells became tempered with something more primal—damp and cold and musty.

"It sucks when it rains topside," Jerica said. "As above, so below. Water finds cracks and crevices and seeps down here. You can't shake the chill loose, so most people spend part of their play deka in the baths. That's a ten-hour cycle—we do everything in ten-hour cycles here. We don't really have days in the Warrens. It's more like everything revolves around a thirty-hour schedule—you work, you play, you sleep."

A group of laughing young people pounded down the wooden basement stairs. They were mostly naked, with towels on their shoulders. They all had long hair, and they all had ribbons tied into random little braids. The teens called out to Jerica as they opened the door and traipsed through.

That was when Quinn Saint Nicholas raised his sleepy, cowlicked head and decided to start playing the game. Max nearly pumped his fist in the air.

First, Quinn murmured, "Well, that explains *those* futures." And then he gave Jerica a stern look and said, "Where is Lord Fool?"

A flush climbed Jerica's neck.

"Quinn?" Max asked.

"There are Revelry members *everywhere* down here. The people in lots of colors, with the ribbons? Those are Revelry members. Some of the stuff that I saw... I get it now. These aren't just members of his court. This *is* his court. These are *all* the Revelry. Is Lord Fool alive, Jerica?"

"Wait... did Lord Fool send Revelry members to hurt

Anna?" Max asked. "We know the attackers were Revelry."

"Of course Lord Fool didn't do that," she said. "He's here, and he's fine. Don't ask anything else. You wanted a crowd? There's a crowd that way."

Whether it was a smart idea or not, Max ignored the fact that there was a pissed principality in front of him and fished for more information. "What's with the ribbons?" he said. "Does it help identify their role in the court?"

Jerica didn't answer right away. Just before Max gave up on a response, she said, "There's so much you don't know. And *roles?* The Revelry doesn't have roles. There's only one real leader in the court that I know about, and he's down here with the rest of us. The ribbons are for a million things that the average anarchist would find important. Look," she added and lifted a corner of her beehive hairstyle to show a calico ribbon tied around a lock of hair. "That's because I liberated a cat from a bad caretaker. Assholes don't deserve cats."

The bare bulb above their head flickered and died. They heard a series of loud, exaggerated groans float down the stairway. Jerica grumbled a quick cantrip, creating a white orb of dim light that slowly grew in intensity.

Max tried charging his own light cantrip and failed miserably. "Why is this so difficult down here?" he complained. "Is it because we're underground?"

"Partly. Maybe? I think it has to do with the buildings," Jerica said. "These aren't rehabilitated ruins. A lot of magic in the city is pooled in old buildings with generations of emotional shit baked into them. What sort of trauma will you find in a brand-new suburban house?"

And then Quinn asked, in one of his mild non-sequiturs filled with bomb-like possibilities, "Is the Arcanum meeting today? I remember that."

Jerica just stared at him, frustrated.

"I've already seen it," Quinn insisted. "You're not telling me anything new. I know Rune is looking for allies. He's searching for us. I know things are about to start moving very,

very fast."

"The Arcanum is not meeting today," she said, slowly and quietly.

"Tomorrow," Quinn decided. Then he said, "Hmmm," and then he nodded to himself.

"I know people find you endearing," Jerica said. "And I've heard about how your new adopted family works. But I'll run and hide if you try to collect me as an aunt." She pointed to the basement stairwell. "Down that path. Watch your head. Meet some people. I'll be back in an hour or two to take you to Cornelius. You probably have questions about the elixir he gave you. And when you're ready for a bowel movement, I have a real treat for you—the Shittiest McMansion."

"You're not going to—" *Watch us.* "Stay with us?" Max finished.

She knew what he meant. "There's no need. I already told you not to wander. You've seen the cannibal worms, right? That's nothing. You do not understand how impossibly large this place is, or how dangerous it can be. Neither the guards nor I need to follow you if you try to escape, because you'll be running into the teeth of something worse. Plus, I'm not getting my hair fucking wet. This beehive took an hour to do. So take a break and go bathe. You smell like kidnapping victims."

CHAPTER FIVE
Max

Since neither of them could generate a light cantrip and didn't want to reveal the Slate, they relied on the faint luminance ahead to guide them.

The cellar stairs led to a tunnel with extremely smooth walls and a low ceiling. It ended in a drop. It wasn't until Max lowered himself down the descent that he realized he was climbing into a giant, semi-empty swimming pool's shallow end.

The ground was a gummy blue and white diamond pattern under a low, craggy ceiling. The shallow end was dry and loosely cluttered with chairs, old folding tables, and a massive, massive mound of clothing. Further along, about halfway down the slope to the deep end, the water's edge began. It formed a cool, briny grotto filled with inner tubes and rafts and portable light sources. A dozen or so people swam or talked or floated within it.

"Do you think these are for everyone?" Quinn asked, bending by the pile of clothes. Nothing was new, with styles that ranged through the last few decades. Max picked up one pair of blue jeans and shook them upside down. Sand and twigs pattered to the ground.

Another group of Revelry youth came down the McMansion passage behind them. Two were naked, and the third threw a towel at a friend and began to undress. Their chatter was punctuated with curious looks at Max and Quinn.

"We're new," Max said, trying to sound cheerful. "We heard about the pool."

The three looked at each other, which ended in harmless shrugs. "Three pools, actually," one of them said. "Cold water down there—but it's salt water. Steam room down the passage to the left. But most people talk and hang out in the pool on the right—that's the only place you can use soap, too. Don't fall asleep and drown—ain't no lifeguards to fish your body out later."

Their laughs didn't sound ironic.

When the group moved on, Max began undressing. "Brand would kill me for saying this, but maybe we should split up to learn what we can? We'll check in every half-hour. If anything happens, just start yelling. Do you... you know... *remember* anything about this? Any warnings?"

He asked the last bit because Quinn was frowning, his hands lingering on the hem of his shirt.

"Quinn?" Max prompted. He decided to hide his pants deep in the pile of clothing, not sure what else to do with the Slate. It wasn't so waterproof that it would survive a dunk in water.

"What? No. I mean, I don't think I ever really saw this place at all. Not even as a metaphor."

"Isn't that strange? It doesn't seem like a place you'd forget seeing."

"I know. Whoever built this must be *really* powerful. Do you think anyone would mind if I wore a bathing suit? There must be a bathing suit in this pile."

"Sure," Max said, and didn't push the issue. When it came to personal space and casual nudity, Quinn wasn't as traditionally Atlantean as most people. Max had always assumed it came from Quinn not wanting to trigger prophecies with unexpected skin-to-skin contact. "I can go ahead now if you want a second?"

"Thanks, Max. I'll be okay. I don't think we need to be worried about anyone from the Revelry, but the guards are a different matter. We need to avoid the guards."

"None of the guards have ribbons," Max said. "They aren't Revelry, are they?"

"No," Quinn said. "And that's something else we need to figure out."

Max hesitated. "Why did you ask about an Arcanum meeting? That's something you remember?"

"It's complicated."

Max tried not to roll his eyes. "Okay. But why is knowing it important?"

"Because we have more time than we think before we have no time at all," Quinn said. "Do you want to start with the pool on the left or right?"

If Max had learned anything about Quinn, it was when to stop pushing. Max backed away from the pile of clothing. "I'll go left—I think that's the steam room. You can check out this pool here, then we'll meet at the pool on the right."

"Thirty minutes. Ish," Quinn promised.

Promising himself he'd check up on Quinn in twenty, assuming he could tell the time, Max set off down the deep-end slope.

The water was so cold it sent a spasm of shock through his body. It was dark and brackish, with the silt-heavy feel of ocean water. By the time he reached the bottom, the water was nearly at his waist.

He waded over to an archway dug from the far left corner of the pool, using the floating platforms and empty rafts for handholds. The dozen or so splashing people in this room were engaged in whorls of conversation and paid him little attention. At least Quinn would have his choice of people to eavesdrop on.

The archway led to a smooth stone ramp that rose above the waterline and had much higher ceilings. Yet again, this odd mix of... Construction? Was that the right word? These tunnel walls were not naturally formed. The sides of the pool were fused into the formation, like a melting photograph. The passage had clearly been created with magic.

He started shivering as he waded up the ramp and out of the bracing water. The moisture in the air warmed almost immediately, though, and thickened with clouds of passing steam. As another archway appeared ahead, the slope peaked and began to lead downwards.

The second pool area had no standing water and lots of random seats. The cherry tops of hot-rock braziers glinted through the steam. Visibility was so poor that Max found an empty chaise lounge and sat for a moment. He used his fae ability to toughen a membrane over his eyes. It made it easier to stare at things without constantly blinking.

What to do first?

There was a young woman near him, lying on her own chaise lounge. She ran a hand through her hair and tugged on a snarl. A bug fell out, which she flicked away with a sigh. She might be someone to talk to.

Further—on the decline leading up to the steam room's shallow end and not the archway to the third pool—was a group of people sitting in a dense arrangement of braziers. The steam around them was as impenetrable as cotton batting. Two people there had ribbons in their hair and the other…

The other wore a paint-splattered camo jacket. He was not just a guard—he was the guard Quinn had warned him about when they first arrived. The redhead.

Max spotted a hand-off between Camo Guy and a Revelry member. Drugs maybe? *Interesting.*

He got up, stretched, made a show of pacing along the bottom of the waterless deep end. After a few meandering minutes, he passed by the young woman and said, "Hey. Have an extra water, by any chance? Or know where I can get one?"

He didn't expect a surprised expression. Flustered, the woman said, "Well, I mean… I suppose you can have a sip. Are you new?"

"I am very new," Max agreed, wondering what he'd said wrong. "Sorry! I left my water bottle in my room."

"Oh. Sure. It's just that people don't really share their bottled water. But there are barrels of it in the lunchroom. It's rainwater, though they boil it first. Tastes like crap, but it'll keep you alive."

Mounds of scavenged clothes and no bottled water? In the back of Max's head, he heard the dry words of his grandmother's daily lessons. Back from the days when she thought he was worth teaching.

"You're not Motley, are you?" the woman added. "I mean, you're not... I mean, you're not one of the..." She flushed with the discomfort of her words. "Do you live in the Warrens?"

"I'm friends with Jerica," he said.

"*Oh*," she said in a gust of relief. "Good. I thought you were from one of the, you know, gangs."

"I didn't even know there were gangs down here. Are they the ones dealing drugs? I kind of hoped there wouldn't be any dealers down here. I'm trying to stay clean."

He pointed his chin up the ramp to the shallow end.

"I wouldn't worry about that," she said. "The drugs are only there for people who go looking for them. Don't get caught using the Agonies anywhere the Lady can see. She doesn't like when people act messy in public."

"The Agonies," Max said. He'd heard about those. Strong stuff that tore up your body in the process. "Damn. I hope I don't see anyone doing those."

"Folks usually go deeper into the Eidolon to use. Just don't try it yourself without asking where it's safe. If you get too far away from the chalets, there's some insane shit. I know someone who got mauled by a bear. And some leftover gangs in the older areas still have tolls and slavery and stuff like that."

"Why still?" Max asked. At the woman's confused blink, he added, "You said there are *still* some gangs left."

"Well, I mean, most of them work for her now. They're not very friendly, but at least they patrol and keep us safe from shit."

And deal drugs. And enforce Lady Time's will. What did it mean that most of them *worked* for her? He had a hard time believing their real purpose had anything to do with keeping people safe.

"Did you say bears?" he asked on a spit-take.

"My friends think they hitched a ride with the translocation and then bred like crazy. Just... don't go sightseeing. People who do that vanish all the time."

The woman excused herself after that, saying she needed to get ready for a work deka. Max took her chair after she left. He pretended to enjoy the steam while watching Camo Guy from half-lidded eyes. The redhead had a bad haircut and a near-solid sheet of freckles.

Max tried to remember where the Agonies came from, but drew a blank. He wasn't even sure that Rune knew. Max seemed to recall the first time Rune or Brand had even heard of them was during their trip to the Green Docks.

As he neared what felt like the fifteen-minute mark, he got up and wandered more. He heard people talking about their shifts. About a rave that was being planned. More than one person came through looking for a friend, and at least one of those people seemed worried.

Eventually, he went through the tunnel leading to the third bath. Just like the first tunnel, it first sloped up over the next room's waterline, then sloped sharply down into it. The water that lapped at his ankles as he descended to the deep end of that pool was neither warm nor cool, covered in a thin film of iridescent soap bubbles, and smelled like chemical flowers.

The Olympic-sized rectangle was filled with many inflated rafts and giant inner tubes, just like the saltwater pool. Someone had lashed dismantled doors to the top of empty multi-gallon plastic drums, creating a free-floating dock. The low ceiling was raw, crystal-studded rock, and the reflection of glow sticks and flashlight beams made Max feel like he was in a sunken grotto crowned with disco balls.

He paddled around for a few minutes and waited for Quinn. Should they have stayed together? Max knew his friend could take care of himself, but *taking care of himself* usually involved prophecy trickery. Feeling suddenly insecure with his decision, Max began swimming to a sloping passage that presumably circled back to that first saltwater pool.

At that moment, his friend poked his head around the corner, saw what there was to see, and headed down the slope toward Max. He'd found a purple bathing suit three sizes too big for him and had a raggedy towel around his shoulders.

"Someone's selling drugs down here," Max whispered when they began to debrief. "I don't know if Lady Time knows. That guy in the camo jacket is one of the dealers. And I hear that people have gone missing. What did you hear?"

"A lot of people are talking about an Ivory soap shortage," Quinn whispered back.

Max stared at him for a moment longer. "I think we should stay in the same room. Let's circulate around here for a while."

So they split up, locally, and went back to paddling or swimming or floating for another twenty minutes, then met on one of the smaller rafts.

They each waited for the other to make a report, which turned into an awkward pause. Finally, Max admitted, "Okay, I heard a lot of people talking about soap, too."

"It's because it floats," Quinn said. "It's harder to lose, and soap is expensive. But I'm not sure it'll help Rune. It feels a bit like a red herring. Did you see any more people dealing drugs?"

"No, but that makes sense. They told me it's kept out of public view, and the steam room is better for sneaky shit. Do you know what the Agonies are?"

Quinn frowned. "Yes. They're awful. Addam gets angry whenever they're mentioned."

"That's the type of drugs they're selling. Did you hear anything else?"

"Yes. People are talking about how weird it is that we're swimming around asking questions," Quinn said. "Oh! And I know where lunch is being served. It's only soup because—"

"Because it's expensive to get food down here, right?" Max finished.

"Does that seem strange?" Quinn asked.

"Only if you're asking yourself what kind of a leader Lady Time is," Max said. "Space? Plenty of space around here. Cheap food. Scavenged goods. But anything with a real cost is hard to get, like bottled water. My grandmother taught me some of this stuff. The value of everything around here is a mirage. It's not a lasting model. My grandmother may have been evil, but she knew enough to care for her foot soldiers. It kept people loyal in the long run."

"People seem happy, though," Quinn said.

"Sure. They have plenty of room to camp out and live. There's a system for them to take care of each other. And Lady Time is providing protection—or at least that's what she'd probably claim. This is the perfect camp. That's what it feels like—not a home, but a camp. A…" Max struggled for the word. Tried to imagine what Rune would say. He settled on, "A staging ground."

Quinn chewed on his lower lip. He must have done some private math in his head, because he finally nodded.

"Yesterday, you said that we had time right now, but it was going to run out," Max said. "What happens next?"

"The thing that always happens when you no longer need a staging ground," Quinn said quietly. "The fight starts."

"So how much time do we have?"

"It's… not always clear. And I can't see it, I can only remember what I saw, which means that maybe it has already changed. But I know the Arcanum comes together—I saw them, or a group of people that *felt* like them. Rune was very interested in a fountain, which is a weird detail, but true. And that meeting is the beginning of the end—whatever is decided there starts the chain of events for this trial."

"Trial?"

"That's how I think about it sometimes. Rune has trials ahead of him. This was always coming. And now I don't know when I can say anything, and when I can't, so I may really be screwing the world up by talking about it."

It was not an average warning, and Quinn wasn't an average Atlantean. It seemed like such a big responsibility for his friend's shivering, narrow shoulders.

"Okay," Max said slowly. "I'm going to do one more lap through the steam room. Then we'll go wait for Jerica by the clothes. Do you want to come with me?"

"No. I'll circle the other way. I'll be alright."

Max lowered himself off the raft and swam back to the steam room passage.

He lingered on the sloping threshold between the pool and the tunnel, running his hands along the slick, melted magic that had formed it. It reminded him a little of Ciaran. Ciaran had a weird ability to turn substances into something that addressed his whims.

But why did someone *build* the Eidolon? It seemed more than a little foolish to bury such a bizarre, intricate compound in—

Oh.

OH.

Max decided that maybe it was time to start asking more questions about Lord Fool's whereabouts.

The steam room didn't hold any new clues, so Max continued the loop back to the saltwater pool. It was just as freezing as before, so he waded into it as quickly as possible. Between the splashing and his angry nerve endings, he almost missed the scene ahead.

On the ramp to the pool's shallow end, just at the waterline, Quinn was confronting—or being confronted by—a guard. One of the friends of the mean-looking redhead.

The guard, with an ugly smile, grabbed the waistband of Quinn's bathing suit and tried to pull it down.

Max stalked forward. It should have been a clumsy, wading gait, but his near-immediate anger fueled his abilities. His body… reacted? He felt strength flowing into his calves and thighs, his subtle shapeshifting giving him the force he needed to cut through the resistance. He was too furious, though, to wonder at the newness of the sensation.

The guard stubbornly held his ground, although his jaw went slack at the suddenness of Max's appearance.

"Mind stepping away from my friend?" Max asked.

"Maybe?" the man said sullenly. "No rule against talking."

"That's good," Max said. "Because if you were doing more than talking to him, I'd name every bone in your body as I broke it. Back the fuck up."

The guard gave Max a cool smile, shrugged, and left by climbing out of the shallow end into the passage back to the McMansions.

Quinn refused to meet Max's eyes. His discomfort had dissolved into an embarrassed look, which was so much worse.

"Hey. I shouldn't have left," Max said gently. "No more splitting up."

"Really, Max, it was just… I mean, he was just teasing me, and I…" Quinn trailed off.

Max was missing something here—whatever caused this rare awkwardness. But this wasn't the place to talk about it, so Max did all he could—he put a hand on Quinn's shoulder and hoped it helped steady him.

"I feel blind," Quinn whispered. "I feel like I'm blindfolded."

"Let's go back to our room. I remember the way. Okay?"

He waited until Quinn nodded. They separated, gathered their things, and began to retrace their steps.

CHAPTER SIX
Max

Quinn wanted to take a nap after they'd navigated back to their guest cell. Max let him, even though he had a feeling Quinn just wanted space, which made Max want to give him the exact opposite.

He forced himself to go outside. The courtyard—*cavern?* Whatever it was, it was quiet. The staff had finished their daily cleaning and moved on to another area of the mansion. Max put together a small exercise area using whatever heavy objects he could drag over, and trained.

He continued to turn matters over in his head. Or at least, he kept thinking of Quinn, which may not have been the immediate emergency but felt like one.

Max had met Quinn over a year ago, during a barbecue behind Half House, Rune and Brand's old home. Quinn excitedly introduced himself as Max's very best friend, with the exception of that one time in the future when they were deadly rivals (or at least Quinn's version of deadly rivals, which had something to do with Max rubbing a ferret in Quinn's hair). Max hadn't been sold on the friend concept at first. Quinn was related to Addam, and Addam was an ass.

Things had changed since then.

Rune was a brother now, not the source of a crush. And Addam managed to smooth Rune's edges, which made Max like Addam more. Plus, Quinn didn't only insist he was Max's friend, he *acted* like it. Right from the start. Literally, from the start, from the very beginning, Quinn planted himself in Max's corner and refused to move.

Had Max done enough to deserve it? He didn't even know why Quinn was distraught. What kind of friend could be so clueless about why his best friend was upset?

"You hate push-ups," Quinn said from the doorway of the converted solarium. "You only do them when you're angry."

Max collapsed to the blanket he'd stretched out on the hard ground. It smelled like cheap detergent. "Yeah."

Quinn came over and sat cross-legged on the edge of the blanket. "So?" he nudged.

Max took a quick, deep breath. "Can we talk about what happened at the baths? About what upset you?"

Interest in the conversation fled Quinn's face. "Maybe later? Let's talk about what we learned."

From his prone position, Max squirmed upright so that they were both at eye level. "Quinn," he said. "Please talk to me."

"There's nothing to talk about. I think the guard was just trying to make me uncomfortable."

"I know, and the way he teased you made you really unhappy."

"I'm fine. Who do you think—"

Max scooted forward until they were barely a foot apart. He didn't know how to express what he felt, that he was upset that Quinn had been hurt, and how angry he was that he hadn't realized that Quinn *could* be hurt this way. And *why*. So he did what Rune usually did when his words and emotions got bottle-necked—he whipped a vow around his head like a morning star.

"Quinn Saint Nicholas, your fights are my fights, your fights are my fights, *your fights are my fights*." For just a second, he felt the air go heavy in his lungs, a ripple of magic leaving his body. "Do you understand me? You are my best friend, and I am so lucky to have you. But someone really upset you, and I don't exactly know why, and that makes me feel awful. I did a shitty job looking out for you."

"You are my best friend too," Quinn said back, and his eyes got glassy. But he was smiling. "I promise. It's nothing, Max. I just... I'm not like..." Quinn fidgeted. "I'm not very Atlantean sometimes."

"Why? Just because you don't want to get naked all the time? Quinn, you are *more* Atlantean than most people I know. You're a fucking Atlantean rock star."

"Not anymore," Quinn said. He chewed on his lip—a clear sign he was about to try to change the subject. "Has Jerica been by? We can go visit the alchemist."

Max folded his arms and waited.

"It's not something you can fight," Quinn said evasively. "There's nothing for you to fight for me."

"Fuck that," Max said. "I will fight anything that makes you feel like this. I don't care if it's a person or a bad mood or whatever. Is there something you're worried about telling me? You've seen *how* many futures, Quinn—do I ever turn away from you in any of them? Do not mention the ferret."

A smile flickered across his face. "No. None of you do. The four of us are meant to be a team. Almost always."

"...Four?" Max said.

"Hopefully," Quinn sighed. "I don't want to jinx anything. It's taking him forever to show up. But Anna is here. And she's getting older. Just wait until you see what she'll become."

"I can't tell if you're trying to change the subject again. Won't you at least tell me why you were so upset?"

Quinn shrugged, but made the serious face he usually did when he planned on answering. His lips worked around a few failed words before he finally said, "There are a lot of people having sex around here. It's very casual. And the guard today, he was teasing me. And he didn't listen when I said no."

"You don't have to have sex with anyone you don't want to. You know that, right? And yes, that is something I can fight. I can damn well freaking fight anyone who tries to make you do something like that."

"Anyone, Max," Quinn said, and there was so much emotion in those words. "I don't want... It's not something that..."

And his face shut down completely.

Max waited a few seconds and said, "If you aren't ready to have sex, then that's the way it is. Just because we live in a horny city doesn't mean you have to do anything you don't want to do."

"What if I'm never ready?" Quinn whispered.

"Do you *want* to be ready?" Max asked.

Quinn blinked at that, surprised.

"Because that's okay, too," Max said. "It always will be. It's your choice."

Quinn's lips tugged up in a smile.

"And I'd like to circle back to the number *four*," he said. "And Anna. I've already figured out she will be a world-class ass-kicker. Do *not* tell her that, though. She can change the world when she's older, let's not feed her ego now."

"She's already changed the world," Quinn said. "But only Layne noticed. I don't think I'm supposed to mention that yet, though. And maybe we shouldn't think about Anna right now. Her magic is wickedly intuitive, and we probably don't want her to follow us."

"Is that Anna Dawncreek?" Jerica asked from the kitchen doorway. Both Max and Quinn turned and answered with a shuttered look that they finally must have got right, because Jerica took a surprised step back. "Shit. That's a hot button."

"You don't ask about our family," Max said. "Not until you decide if you're a good guy or not."

"I'm not a bad guy," Jerica said angrily.

"That's not enough," Quinn said.

Max said, "We want to see Cornelius now."

What they said must have bothered her, because she simmered on it while leading them through Lady Time's mansion. They went in a new direction, through a series of rich, moldering hallways and stairways that grew less ornate and more utilitarian until finally, they were more or less walking through concrete corridors in the basement.

"You *know* I can't say certain things," Jerica finally exploded. "This is her compound. She is Arcana. It's her game."

"You're a *principality*," Max shot back.

"In the twenty-first century, yeah," she said. "Lady Time is a fucking Big Bang Arcana. You have no idea how strong she is. I cannot stop her, I can only help the people I've sworn to help."

"So that's what this is?" Max said. "You're not helping Rune because you want to help the Revelry? Do you think Rune wouldn't want to help them either? There's obviously something wrong there—no one will talk about Lord Fool."

"Did it ever occur to you that I am helping Rune by not telling you something that will encourage you to act like a stupid teenager?" When Max tried to argue, she held up a hand and refused to speak more.

It wasn't much later that they stopped before a giant, steel-buttressed door. Jerica rapped on one of the metal panels with a closed fist.

"He'll make us wait," she grumbled.

Max dialed back on the more pointed questions he wanted to ask and said, "So you're Revelry? Your bloodline?"

"No one is Revelry," she said. "It's a concept, not a lineage." She gave Quinn a grudging nod. "My blood has more in common with him than anyone else here."

"Me?" Quinn said in surprise. He rolled his eyes up to the ceiling thoughtfully. "Did I know that?"

"Do you pay much attention to your paternal line?" she asked back.

"Oh no. It's all maternal in my mom's court. So you're Nightglade?" Quinn saw the look on Max's face and laughed. "Well, I had to have a father, didn't I? What did you think?"

"I thought your father was in your court too."

"He is one of my mom's husbands. I think it started as a business alliance with Lady Moon? He moved back to the Nightglade when I was a baby."

He skipped over the last bit quickly. Quinn had been sickly as a child. Between that and a gift for prophecy, his own mother had even effectively cut him from the family portrait. Max hadn't realized Quinn's father had ostracized him too. *A whole new person to hate*, Max marveled.

A metal clank silenced them, followed by grinding, squealing gears. The door began to slide into a recess.

The alchemist waited on the other side, hands folded calmly against his stomach. He wore a simple robe and thin sandals. Max tried not to stare at his face, but it was so damn unusual to see people that old in New Atlantis. Rune's notes had been maddeningly vague on the subject, but Lady Time had been unable to rejuvenate. Was Cornelius unable to rejuvenate too? There was something about that that Rune refused to talk about.

"How nice," Cornelius beamed. "You've got your color back, Quinn. That was a quick recovery—some prophets take days."

"I do feel much better," Quinn said, cheerful and polite. *Too* cheerful. "Thank you."

"I'll leave you here," Jerica said. "Please go right back to your room. I'll meet you there in an hour."

As she left, Cornelius said, "Follow me, then. We'll chat over biscuits."

There were a series of rooms on the other side—dingy and poorly-lit, crowded with both the junk from someone else's life and boxes and crates of alchemy equipment. It looked prosaic and efficient.

It also made Max's skin crawl. He was sensitive enough to magic to know that things in this basement were not as they appeared. Even Cornelius seemed to shimmer in front of his eyes.

Quinn, still in an odd, faux-cheerful mood, peppered Cornelius with questions. Max lingered by a worktable, where different reagents were laid out. (And he liked how quickly that word came to his tongue: reagents. He'd picked up a few things from the fae alchemist Ewa.) He bent low and eyed a waxy substance pressed into a little ball.

"Ah," Cornelius said, looking over at Max. He was showing Quinn a tray of fruit. "That's one of my most expensive ingredients. Took me days of research to find it. Hard to find Atlanteans with the right medical condition—I had to import from America."

"What is it?" Max asked.

"Dandruff from the scalp of a jaundiced hemophiliac. The oil balance is especially important, or else you can't sculpt it into little pellets."

Max stepped away from the petri dish.

"As I was saying," Cornelius announced. "Lady Time does like infusing strawberries with her potions when required. But the potency leaches away too quickly. I think something like a grape, with a tougher skin, may be warranted."

"Fascinating," Quinn said. "It's so creative."

"I'd like to talk about the poison you gave Quinn," Max interrupted. "Can we talk about that?"

Cornelius laughed. "I'd hardly call it poison."

"You took away one of his natural gifts without his permission. I could call it a lot worse than poison."

"It was hardly without his permission. I doubt young Quinn has allowed much to happen in his life without his permission."

"Well, I wasn't *particularly* happy about enrolling into Magnus Academy," Quinn said. "I even kicked sand in the direction of my brother when he told me. Not *at* him, of course. But it all worked out."

Max stared at Quinn for a beat. He was being nice to Cornelius for a reason.

"I do have some questions, though," Quinn said. "About

the potion. I've taken potions before to try to... Hmm. To try to smooth the edges of my gift? Nothing worked very well."

"Undisputedly," Cornelius agreed. "Modern formulae are weak and insufficient to mute gifts like yours. But Lady Time comes from an era rich with prophets. Alchemical intervention was more researched and resourced then. She brought this secret with her."

"Will the potion wear off?" Max asked bluntly.

Max watched Quinn's eyes close and open—a brief blink of pain.

Cornelius made thoughtful sounds of consideration as he put the tray of fruit back into a small refrigerator. "Yes? No? That's beyond the scope of Lady Time's immediate cares. As Quinn likely knows."

He closed the fridge door and turned to face Quinn fully.

"Do you know what your future holds, if your gift were allowed to grow unfettered? I'd like to try something. Stay right where you are, and do not look at Max. Max, say nothing. Understood?"

Quinn turned, so his back faced Max. Max saw Quinn's shoulders hitch uncertainly.

"Is Addam alive, Quinn?" Cornelius asked.

"Is— Of course Addam is alive!"

"Truly? Or are you simply remembering one of the timelines where he survived? Can you tell me, right here and now, if you remember whether your brother is alive in the fixed, present-day timeline?"

"Of... of course..." Quinn whispered. His voice rose. "Addam is alive!"

"His death would have devastated you. Are you sure this isn't one of those potential futures where he died, and you simply prefer to remember those futures when he lived?"

"He's *alive!*" Quinn cried. "Right? Max right? Right?" Now he turned, desperate.

"He's alive and well and burning a path toward you," Max whispered. He turned his gaze on Cornelius. Sometimes there were no other words that summed up a situation better than a low, fierce, "Fuck you."

Cornelius held out his hands. "This is what his future will hold if his gift returns and grows. Madness. Uncertainty. A lack of connection with the real world."

Quinn, no longer facing Cornelius, closed his eyes while he calmed down. Finally, he manufactured another light, bright smile, and turned back to the alchemist. "That was a clever analogy. Thank you for sharing it. Was this a very difficult potion to make? It seems frightfully difficult."

Quinn began to circle toward the opposite side of the table, drawing Cornelius's attention with him. He held his arm low and surreptitiously made the hand signal for an air ambush. Then he balled it into a fist, as if reconsidering his absolute shit memory for the hand signals that Brand told him he needed to study more, and made the gesture for a fast retreat to home base.

Max already figured out Quinn was buying him a moment to be nosy, so he turned and walked around the L-shape in the basement.

The more he saw of the lab, the more he realized it wasn't a permanent fixture. Most of the supplies were in boxes or canvas bags, and a standing lamp supplemented the plain bulbs overhead.

There were two doors, both ajar. One was a storage room, filled with the sort of crap that any old basement was filled with. The other had medical gurneys and medical supplies. *A clinic?* There were no patients, though Max saw a bag of clothing in one corner. The reddish bags were industrial-strength plastic—the type you saw containing biohazard material. He stepped into the room quickly and opened the flap of one. He smelled shit and sweat and dried blood.

There were a lot of clothes in that one bag, and from this angle, he spotted two other bags piled in a corner.

In the other room, Quinn raised his voice and said, "Isn't that right Max?"

Max hot-footed it back to the front room, saying, "Sorry, missed that. And if Lady Time is so great, why can't she build you a better lab? A battle alchemist deserves more."

Cornelius's head snapped up. He covered his surprise with a beneficent smile. "Not many people know that term. And this is just an… auxiliary lab. I have much better ones. In fact, I'll be returning to one of them after dinner. I hear that guests might be on the way."

"We'll leave you to it, then," Max said. "Thank you for seeing us."

When they had a full stairway between them, Max started relaxing. "Did you want to kick him in the nuts as much as I did? That was a mean trick he pulled on you."

"It's alright," Quinn said. "He gets caught in a blizzard. It's hard to be angry at him. Did you see anything in the lab?"

"I did, but let's go back to that blizzard comment for a second."

"Hmm?" Quinn gave him that smile he always did when he was buying himself a few seconds so that he could decide if he was over-sharing. "It's just a metaphor. It used to be for Rune or Brand, but now it can mean Addam too. They blur together, and when they get angry, all I see is static. Like a white-out? Or a blizzard? The three of them do rage really, really well."

"So Rune meets Cornelius?"

"Or Addam or Brand, I think. I saw it right before he gave me the potion. But what did you *find*, Max?"

"A bunch of clothes."

"Like the clothes at the pool?"

"Like clothes people leave behind when they're maybe too dead to wear them? My gut is telling me that we should learn more about where these missing people have gone. What if—"

His jaw clicked shut a half-second before his brain sifted through the signals that were warning him someone was waiting around a corner in front of him.

In the ransacked kitchen of the mansion, the guard in the camo jacket blocked the door to the courtyard.

He just stood there, flat-eyed and calm.

Quinn halted a step behind Max, giving Max the first response. Max decided to wait and see whether this would turn into a fight.

There was a phrase that people use: *someone with dead eyes*. It wasn't just a literary metaphor. Brand explained it to Max once. Some psychopaths were less polished than others and forgot to crinkle their eyes when they mimicked human expressions. Like the smile that Camo Guard slowly slid over his face.

"Just wanted to make sure you were doing alright," he said, and stepped away from the door. "Some of us are keeping tabs on you. For your protection."

"I have three Arcana in my contact list," Max said. "I do not need your protection."

"But you can't contact them now, can you?"

Max just smiled, gave a quick *let's-go* tilt of the head to Quinn, and continued to their room.

CHAPTER SEVEN
Max

One of the McMansions had been stripped to the floorboards, then filled with anything that could approximate a table: coffee tables, round barstool tables, folding tables, banquet tables, even giant real-wood monstrosities that must have taken a dozen people to lift.

Jerica had brought Max and Quinn to a community meal shared by second-shift dekas. By this point in their captivity, they'd lost all concept of time. After Quinn's day-long recovery, the thirty-hour cycles made it more confusing.

They sat at the smallest table they could find in the smallest room—maybe it was a closet, actually? But they had a bit of privacy while discreetly curious Revelry members passed by the closet door and sat at a wrought-iron patio table in the empty master bedroom. Jerica said she'd fetch them in an hour.

"I can't believe it's midnight," Max whispered. "It feels like morning."

"We're running out of time," Quinn said. "Everything starts happening today."

"Because you remembered that Rune bitched about a fountain yesterday?"

"I still don't understand that, but Rune should be on the move. The Arcanum should be acting. And so will Lady Time. I don't think we have much time left down here—I just know there's something we can find. Something we need to find."

Max dragged his spoon through the bowl of soup. It was

mainly broth—and not one type of broth, but a mishmash of random canned broth. There were some rough, chopped vegetables, too, softened to the point of mush by over-boiling, and flecks of grayish meat. But it was still nutrition, and no one had to pay for it.

"You heard those people in line talking about a demonstration, right?" Max said.

"They seemed nervous about it," Quinn said.

"It's above ground. I don't think many of them want to go back above ground."

"Why would they?" Jerica asked, swooping into the closet with a small plate of machine-sliced bread. There was a scoop of butter substitute on the side.

"I thought you weren't coming back for a while?" Max asked.

"Plans changed," she said vaguely.

"Do you know what this above-ground demonstration is?" Quinn asked. "Or *when?*"

Jerica shrugged a yes-no-maybe.

Max nibbled on the bread. It had a sawdusty, expired taste. He put it back down.

"Not up to your cook's menu?" Jerica asked.

"We don't have a cook. We have a family member who cooks for us. Why do you keep baiting us? Why are we your enemy?"

"You're not my enemy," she said in exasperation.

"Then why are you protecting her?"

"I am not protecting her, either," Jerica said. "I'm just trying to keep the Arcanum from blundering in and ruining everything."

"Jerica, Lady Time has *slaughtered people*," Max hissed, lowering his voice at the end. "She slaughtered them and stole their sigils like some fucked-up ancient battlefield. Did you see her share those sigils with anyone? She is not after anyone's best interest but her own. She's bringing war with her."

"Then battle her! Above ground!" Jerica responded in the

same shout-whisper. "Don't destroy the Eidolon and what it represents. I know you see a lot of people from the Revelry, and I know Lord Fool tried his best to care for them, but more and more people find us every day. People whose only homes were dark, dirty hallways in the Warrens. People whose day-to-day existence was mired in disease, hunger, abuse. Look around you! Just... just look at what is in your field of vision! Everyone worked to find tables from other parts of the Eidolon and dragged them here. To create a space for *free food*. What has happened here is *working*. We're finding a way to shelter and protect people who have always had to fend for themselves. I don't want this destroyed."

"Why can't you separate Lady Time from the Eidolon?" Max asked in rising frustration. "They aren't the same thing!"

"And how is the Arcanum any better? Do you honestly think Lord Tower spends his days worrying about collateral damage? That he wouldn't hesitate to boil the baby in the bathwater?"

Max looked at Quinn, wondering if he'd jump in with another convenient prophetic memory. But Quinn appeared busy either listening or pulling a wayward hair off his tongue.

What would Rune do? What would Rune say? There was so much information here, Max just didn't know how to fish for it.

So he threw all that together in his head and asked himself what he really, really wanted from his argument. And the answer was there: he didn't want Fiddler Blue to be a bad guy. Which gave him an idea.

"If you care so much about the people down here, why aren't you upset that some of them have gone missing?" Max asked bluntly.

Jerica leaned back in her chair. Her angry expression washed out into wariness.

"People are missing. Quinn and I learned that in a single day—so you must be aware, too."

"People come and go," Jerica said, her Adam's apple sliding

up and down in a nervous movement.

"You just said people are coming. That word of the Eidolon is drawing people in. So why would people go?"

"Drug use is—"

"No. No, it's more than that. People are *missing*, and they have friends walking around looking for them. Did you know there are bags of old clothing in the alchemist's lab—Cornelius's lab?"

"We have *tons* of used clothing lying around. Most of it came with translocations, or were donated by thrift shops."

"The clothes in the lab smelled like death. Like blood."

Jerica's complexion went ashen. She stared down at her plate of bread and said nothing.

"I don't think you're a bad person, but you need to start asking better questions," Max said. "We're not looking to take the Eidolon away from people. We're not looking to unmake whatever is being made here. But whatever Lady Time wants from all of you, it's not what you think."

Jerica's pocket beeped. She pulled out an old digital Ms. Pac-Man watch. "We may have an answer to that soon. She's..." Jerica hesitated, and then her expression firmed. "She'll make an appearance soon. She will invite you to dinner. Play nice, boys. Please play nice with her. I'll look into what you said—but do *not* show your hand in front of her. She is not safe." The last was barely a whisper. "Do you understand?"

They finished their food quickly, and put their plates in plastic tubs. By the time they moved to the second-floor stairway, people were already reacting to Lady Time's off-stage arrival.

In an actual mansion, the balcony over the central hall rotunda would have been a nice art gallery, with lots of wall space. But everything was scaled so small that there was barely enough room for people to crowd the banisters and look down at Lady Time.

She worked her way into a mob of people, hands serenely clasped together, nodding at the excited and nervous comments she received.

Finally, she raised her voice.

"Very soon, we will march to the surface and make our presence known. It's time for the city to learn that a new force has gathered. It's time we stop telling the stories of Queens and Kings. It's time we give the pawns their due.

"Tell me, my friends: what have they offered you before now? What has their leadership done for you?" She threw her hands up, speaking to the people on the second floor. "They lead you into battles. They place you on the front lines. It is a drama of their own making, and none of it—*none of it!*—changes the fact that we need to eat, and raise our children, and laugh with friends. Why can't we be allowed to do this without their maddening excess? Why must we starve and sleep in the dirt to support their wasteful, elite ways?"

The words stirred up a storm of cheers and shouts and complaints, as Max knew they were meant to do.

"Rest and be ready. Before the sun sets on another day, we will come together and march to the streets of New Atlantis. Once there, under my protection, our voices will finally rise as one. No one will fail to hear or see us!"

She drank in their reaction. Her eyes flicked upwards and landed on Max and Quinn. She smiled at them, and headed toward the stairway upwards.

"Looks like we've got plans," Max murmured.

The first thing Lady Time said, one quiet walk later, as the door closed to her personal dining room, was: "I thought we provided baths to deal with that wretched stink."

The table was set with cream-colored silk, mismatched ceramic plates, and platters of food far better than the soup they'd just eaten. Max and Quinn were seated along with the three principalities that orbited Lady Time: Jerica, the alchemist Cornelius, and Vadik Amberson. Vadik was dressed in his ostentatious green leathers, but his hooded mask hung over his back.

In addition to Lady Time's inner circle was one guest that made Max nervous. He'd changed from his camo jacket into a plain brown shirt and combed his red hair.

"I'll see what I can do about it," Cornelius murmured. "Perhaps while I'm tending to matters in the Warrens today, my apprentice Maon can assist."

The smug look on the young guard's face indicated that this, then, was Maon. Was he an alchemist too? A fae alchemist. Max had a sinking feeling he knew what court Maon had belonged to, which might have explained his constant glares at Max.

"By all means," Lady Time said. "Let's clear the lowest bar I could set for battle alchemists. Soap." She changed the subject with a flick of her fork. "Is the Waylan fellow organizing the raff for the march topside? I want no dissent. Their presence on the street is essential."

"Yesterday, you asked us to find Waylan and kill him," Vadik said, in a neutral tone that bordered on bland.

"Did I?" Lady Time noted. "He does vex, doesn't he? His purpose will be outlived soon enough. Fine. Fiddler Blue, I expect you to keep the mob in line, then."

"You want to kill Juror Waylan?" Quinn blurted out.

"Want?" she echoed.

Quinn's blurt spread into a red blush. "He does seem to be important to the future of the city, if I remember correctly."

"That timeline has died, little scion," Lady Time said.

"But—"

She held up a hand. Quinn's teeth clicked. She said, "His death will serve my interests. I'm not sure I can put that any clearer. These are the realities of ruling."

She lowered her eyes to the rare steak in front of her.

With methodological precision, she began to cut out bite-sized pieces, yet didn't actually eat any of them. After each saw of the knife, she paused, and magic surged over her plate.

Everyone got quiet and focused on their own food. Max didn't know what had happened—or why it was a performance. But it was absolutely a performance. It was absolutely a show of power.

When she was done cutting every bit of food into forkfuls, the magic began to surge a different way—a release of some sort. It *felt* like a release to Max, at least. She was releasing the magic before every bite of food she began to take.

That was when he realized she was, without any sort of obvious sigil to assist her, putting each bite into stasis. She was holding every single bite's warmth and flavor with time magic. Max was not as well versed in the different disciplines of magic as Rune was, but judging from the side-eye from the principalities, this was not something the average Atlantean could do. Or should do.

"My Lady," Jerica said politely after several minutes of awkward silence and clinking silverware. "I have a request, if I may?"

Lady Time waved a fork at her.

"Our exploratory teams think they've discovered another wing of the Eidolon," Jerica continued. "They're working to break into it, but sigil magic would be useful. Perhaps, just this once, I could bring some of my own into the Eidolon? Or borrow some from your armory?"

"Sigils," Lady Time said. "In the hands of my soldiers?" She raised her knife, slick with blood from her steak, and placed it against her jugular. "Shall I give them the blade at my throat, too?"

"Of course not," Jerica said, and dropped her eyes. "It was a foolish question."

Lady Time smiled around the table—well, not a smile. It was all stage acting. Max could practically hear Brand bark in his ear, *Now is when you keep your mouth shut and let the stupid bad guy explain every stupid element of their stupid life-plan-slash-life-story.*

"There were other things I wished to discuss. I thought it best if our guests became better acquainted with me. My mandate to rule, you see," Lady Time said, "was interrupted. Long ago. Now I claim reparations, which will be no simple thing. Nothing is simple when the wills of gods are thwarted." She lifted her wine glass and took a small sip. "And make no mistake, I come from a family of gods. The secrets we uncovered—our mastery of time magic—made us nearly untouchable. How else could I have survived an entire life cycle in the timestream?"

"You lived in the timestream," Quinn said. "*Lived* in it? I didn't think it was the sort of thing one could live in."

"One doesn't. By choice. My father saw no other escape when he pulled me into it. Our jealous peers were all but dragging the gallows noose to our estate doors. At that point, circumstances had conspired to make him... push the boundaries of time magic. Done something no one else could—saved the lives of three of his children. The other Arcana were scared and came for him."

She put down her silverware and leaned back in the chair. She stroked threadbare velvet-padded arms. "He'd planned an escape route should political matters decay beyond repair. It is a unique magic—something known only to my line. We call them Moments. Stolen minutes of real time, bottled into an endless loop, donated from the minds of powerful spell casters."

At this, her gaze swooped along the table, landing on each principality with a possessive smile. "But I get ahead of myself. My father fled certain death with me—his true heir. I was barely a child, yet to come into my natural abilities. In what years I had with him afterward, he'd lost much of his mind and never quite confessed what went wrong. Certain rituals anchor us to the real world when we cross into Moments—and if you fail to do that, there is no easy path out. Trust me on that. It took me nearly ninety years to find another route."

"I don't understand how you survived," Quinn said, and

Max caught Quinn's barely subtle aren't-I-very-earnest tone. Quinn was so much sneakier than people admitted.

"Life in a Moment is indescribable. These Moments... they are a slice of existence, eternally looping a bare handful of minutes—five, ten, a half hour. I never found a Moment longer than an hour. But each Moment was filled with constantly replenished resources. Real food and water, shelter for sleep, and even the stunted companionship of real souls. People. Echoes of people who remember their immediate present with unfailing precision, yet forget their own immediate past with every loop. They made for the oddest friends and lovers.

"But everything dies, even memories. Over time the Moments would crack and fade, and my actions within them left damaged tracks. Eventually, I would need to flee to another haven—first with my father and his slow slide into madness, and then on my own as my powers grew. I barely remember the day I left him behind forever, to be honest. It seems so long ago."

"But you found a way out," Quinn finished.

"I found... new friends. Like minds. Powerful minds that could share new Moments with me. And I eventually realized that these connections were all clustered *now*. To this *now*. This handful of years and decades around this so very, very special *now*. I saw these years as a beacon—a forest fire in a world of forests, unique only by the smoke that drew me on. Your little Sun."

"Rune," Max said—the word startled out. He curled his hands into fists, his nails biting at his palm. "Are you talking about Rune?"

"Him and his delicious encounter with your Hanged Man. The Gallows, in this day and age, knew more about time magic than any living person—which isn't saying much, mind you. His grasp of it was brittle and vain. But he knew enough to create damage to the timestream. A lovely little rip that your Sun wandered into—and in which he faced the Hanged Man.

It was only a handful of seconds, but they did it—they stared at each other across time. So while, yes, the Hanged Man created cracks in the timestream—places I could find purchase and widen—it was the force of their initial confrontation that drew me toward them. How apt your master's incarnation."

"You formed bonds with principalities from this time, and they helped you escape," Quinn said, his voice sharper than it had been since he'd taken the potion. "That's what happened, isn't it? Once you knew about the damage to the time stream that Lord Hanged Man did in this era?"

"We didn't—" Jerica said stubbornly, and the look Lady Time turned on her had Max's heart skip a beat.

"Your gratitude will come later, and I will forgive its tardiness," Lady Time said.

But maybe, just maybe, there was a hint of strain in her voice, as if she was growing tired of telling people how great a life of servitude would be under her. Or at least, that was Max's impression.

The table fell into an awkward silence punctured only by the sounds of silverware and ceramic and muffled chewing. Unlike most awkward moments, it didn't dissolve under the weight of passing minutes. Lady Time's irritation grew and grew until she simply pushed her plate away from her in disgust.

"I give you all a chance to see how glory works—the gears and mechanisms behind true power. This could be your future if you learn to adapt. But if you persist in looking backward—"

She suddenly slammed a hand down on her table. The entire corner splintered, sending a section of tablecloth and plates and condiments crashing to the ground.

Magic roared from her—an unrelenting wave of pure ability coalesced in Lady Time's rising Aspect. A low, keening moan filled the air around them. Max should not have been able to understand the sounds, but he did, and it was like understanding the concept of an entire ocean while a single wave swamped you.

It was the sound of giants and epochs—the sound of Saturn's rings; the sound of blue whales; the sound of quasars and black holes and grinding tectonic plates.

The young alchemist—Maon—began to choke. Badly. Fresh blood poured from his lips as he tried to hack up whatever blocked his throat. What finally landed on his plate was not a dead thing. It was bleeding and spasming, a bite of steak no longer resembling steak so much as living tissue and muscle.

"If you ever sit in front of me chewing your cud like that again, I'll put you in the next vat of soup," she whispered.

As her Aspect began to fade, Max saw the tiniest flicker of movement in the corner of his eyes. Trying to keep his head from turning, he watched as Quinn surreptitiously lowered the Magnus slate, which was, Max suspected, recording all audio and visual.

That struck Max as a potentially risky move in the hands of someone who'd spent his life relying on prophecy for unflappable timing.

As Lady Time's head began to snap in Quinn's direction, Max lightly slapped the table with both palms and said, "Is there any dessert?"

They took the dumbwaiter shortcut to their cell. Neither said a single word until they had an entire floor between them and Lady Time.

Quinn was last to crawl out of the shaft into the old kitchen. There must have been cobwebs between his fingers, because he began flapping them.

"That was horrifying. Did she make a bite of cooked meat come to life?" Quinn asked.

"Rune always calls that shit smoke and mirrors," Max said. "But I'm never eating around her again."

They made their way out the door, into the cavern courtyard. The door to the converted sunroom was open, and

Max distinctly remembered closing it. He held up his hand in the *wait* signal and then stared at Quinn until he was sure Quinn knew what the hand signal meant. Quinn nodded.

Inside their room, sitting calmly on a rollaway mattress, was an older man with straggly gray-brown hair and a bushy unibrow. He was nibbling from a plate of French fries that smelled like cold grease. One of his pupils was twice the size of the other.

They stared at each other.

"Hello?" Max said cautiously.

The man scratched his nose, studying them. "Sometimes you figure out where you need to go without me hinting—except for that one time with the lava pit, of course, but really, you should have taken your other right—but Quinn isn't always feeling very clairvoyant, so I thought I'd check and see if you were on your way to the attic yet. She's a brave girl, your Anna, but it's a bad place to wait alone."

Max sat down on a chair. Hard.

"It looks like you're still dawdling," Lord Fool said. "Crooked mansion, attic, chop-chop."

He vanished in a pop of light and shadow.

CHAPTER EIGHT
Anna

"Anna? Anna, are you okay?"

The timid voice roused Anna from wherever her brain had drifted. She was standing by a window on the first floor, looking toward the largest forest on the property.

"Yeah," Anna said, shaking her head. "I was just daydr—"

That's when she noticed Max standing at the edge of the forest—a familiar white-headed blur even at that distance. He was waving at her furtively.

A lot of things occurred to Anna in a very short time.

First, people must assume she's stupid if they'd think she'd believe Max would randomly try to lure her outside during a crisis. Second, her instinct—the instinct tied to her magic—was telling her *it's-okay-but-move-move-move!* Third, she figured any opportunity to investigate would be taken away from her if she told an adult.

"Just daydreaming," Anna said. "I'm going to take a walk outside."

"You were saying that," Queenie said.

"I was?"

Queenie nodded and held out a wrist-watch shaped phone in one hand and a plastic bag of homemade snack mix in another.

"Queenie, stop making us snacks!" Anna said in exasperation. "That is Rune and Brand's stupid boy-programming. We should be making you snacks!"

But she took the bag and phone anyway. It wasn't even an actual phone, just the Magnus Academy device loaded with a bad Facebook clone that all the students had to use.

"Thanks. I'm just going to take a walk," Anna said, as her blood continued to pound *go-go-go-go-go*. "Be right back."

Anna used one of the three best paths to the lawn, easily avoiding the main hall, front doors, and Layne. There were so many different routes you could take - it was like living in a palace - and Anna didn't want to tempt Layne into acting like a babysitter. When Rune had headed to Lord Fool's compound, he'd told Layne to keep an eye on Anna, as if Anna hadn't been the one babysitting Corbie since she was eleven years old.

Dawn had become true morning by then, but the grass outside was still heavy and damp. Anna's sneakers were soaked by the time she reached the edge of the forest.

The person sitting under a shadeless tree looked less and less like Max as she approached. He was a small, thin man with unwashed hair and a grease-stained robe, and he radiated power.

"Are you using magic to trick me?" Anna asked.

"Oh that's almost certainly possible. Isn't it? It's a necessary shortcut."

"You're an Arcana, aren't you?" She thought of which Arcana she'd *not* want to bump into alone. "Crap. You're not Lord Star, are you?"

The man blinked eyes that didn't look the same size, then exploded into giggly laughter. "Oh dear, that was funny. Delicious, even. I'm the first and last of all Arcana—except for the Regency, but they don't like to talk about that. I'm a zero and zilch."

In the human version of tarot cards—themselves cribbed from Atlantean myth—only one major arcana card didn't have a number. That was in the Magnus Academy primer. Anna's heart squeezed painfully in her chest. "You're Lord Fool. Are

Rune and Brand and Addam alright? Are they—"

He held up a firm hand. "I'm not watching *their* story, I'm watching *yours*. The young men aren't very well kitted out. Did you pack what you need, so I can take you to them? I need to get back to my kitchen. I know Francis is messing with the fry machine, which just won't do."

"Did I—?" Alarm raced through Anna. *Young men?* "Are you talking about Quinn and Max? I didn't know I was supposed to bring anything! Do I have time to get my aunt?"

"Just you, child. Your aunts and sibling need to be somewhere else eventually, and it would be... awkward if Brother Sun learns of my tinkering. I suppose you have time to ask three questions, only I mustn't answer the third or fourth. But do hurry. *Francis.*"

There were a lot of people in Rune's orbit who spoke in riddles. Sometimes you just needed to lean into it and talk fast. "What do I need?"

"They have no sigils or money, which will be useful, I dare say."

"Are they hurt? Where exactly are they? Why can't you bring them here? Why me?"

"They've been treated well, but the hospitality is wearing thin. Transporting you into the Warrens—very, very deep in the Warrens—will be easy because you're you. I don't know if it's wise to continue this now. We need to leave in eleven minutes. If we wait more, she may not find you in the bedroom."

Anna had no idea what most of that meant. But there was an Arcana in front of her saying she had eleven minutes to grab money and sigils. She didn't know if she should go, but the smartest course of action was to puzzle it out while doing exactly what the Arcana asked.

She turned and sprinted back to the mansion.

She'd probably never know if magic or luck was at work,

but she made it back outside in eleven and a half minutes without being caught by Layne or Corinne.

The first thing she did was to tamp down the newish Companion bond between her and Corinne, to prevent Corinne from becoming suspicious. It wasn't that difficult. Rune always made it sound like he was slicing his brain in half.

The money was easy. Addam had hidden $10,000 behind a loose panel in the upstairs hallway, so she carefully separated a wad of ten hundred-dollar bills. (Addam had said, *You will use this in emergencies, no questions asked.* Rune had said, *I trust you'll make good decisions.* Brand had said, *This is your fuck-up fund, and wow, will we talk about it afterward.*)

She grabbed a belt of sigils from Quinn's room—which cost a couple of minutes, because she couldn't find his regular leather holster. The one she finally grabbed only had three discs in it.

She also ran by her room. She pulled on a torn and smelly sweatshirt from the laundry hamper, then pried up the floorboard in the closet. She grabbed the knife and darts she'd hidden and stuffed everything into a small trash bag. She also took thirty seconds to jot down as reassuring a note as possible, saying she had an idea to help the dumb boys.

Only when she was racing back to the forest did she finally ask herself if she was making a good decision. Maybe she should at least try to yell for Diana? But the Fool had said *aunts*, and in this new jumbled family, Diana qualified as one of those.

And Rune was out there, right now, fighting to protect his court. Anna was his heir. His actual, declared, one-heartbeat-from-the-throne *heir*. Quinn and Max were *her* people. If she acted useless in an emergency, how was she supposed to ever really be valuable to Rune? Would he or Brand have stood back and not helped—even at her age?

And then there was the fact that everyone thought she was so damn powerful. Why? Because she made a crayon golem for

Corbie once?

She was so wrapped up in her internal argument that she tripped over a branch in the lawn and went sprawling. *Stupid fucking branch*, she yelled, but only inside her brain, because the Corbie-named "Swer Jar" was a real thing. But the eleventh minute was about to become twelve, and there wasn't any time left to whine.

When she arrived, the Fool applauded. "The grass stains are an inspired touch. Inspired! I didn't see the sweatshirt."

Didn't see…? Anna looked down at it. "I figured it would help me blend in if the people underground were all dusty and stuff. I can take it off if things are fancy."

"Inspired," he repeated. "But the dominoes have tipped, little sister. We're already running late. Can I see your phone?"

"My phone? I only have my school phone."

"Perfect," he said, and accepted the Magnus Slate. He ran a hand over the surface. "Science and magic are just two sides of the same eyeball. This connects you to them. Start walking *that* way, and the portal will open when you're close enough. Find a private spot. Sometimes Kellum is nosy and looking out a window, and he spots the glow."

"Kellum?" she said. "Do I know a Kellum?"

The Fool frowned. "Hmm. Wrong probability. It's all so blurry, and I'm distracted, because I just know Francis is going to pour truffle oil into the vat. It's quite frustrating. Aren't you worried that it's almost the twelfth minute? Hurry hurry hurry, Annawan! Lady Time's boudoir won't be empty for long, and you almost certainly want to begin the search there."

Lord Fool handed her the Slate. Anna ran in the direction he had pointed.

She knew a secluded spot, and hoped no one spotted her from the window, because she didn't want to burn this escape route. She had spied on Brand while he cleared a secret motorcycle path through the woods. He'd probably be pissed if he knew she was using it to sneak off the estate.

Not that she came close to reaching the edge of the estate.

A shimmering portal yawned open right in front of her, and she tripped through it with a yelp.

She heard Max cry, "The portal shut already!"

And Quinn said, "I think it's Anna! It has Anna's hair!"

"Stop petting me," she said as the beam of the Slate flashlight bounced around a low-ceilinged room. She tried to climb to her feet, but the floor wanted to make her stumble sideways.

She whispered a light cantrip. The air sparked uselessly. She frowned, got pissed, and pumped more energy into her demand. A grapefruit-sized ball of light appeared above the three of them.

Both boys gaped at the light instead of her, which seemed the less surprising thing. It gave her time to look around. Were they in an attic? Only the floor sloped horribly, and all the attic-type junk was shattered into pieces at the bottom of the slope.

"I guess that settles that," Max whispered, still staring at the light. When he looked down at Anna, there was an expression on his face she couldn't decipher. There was a lot of worry in it, and some awe, and maybe even he was a little happy, because he rushed over and hugged her.

"You're okay?" he whispered.

"Yes. The Fool said I could help." Max's look told her that her presence was not a help at all, though, which stung harder than she'd thought. "*Max*. I can help, really. Don't be mad I'm here. Please?"

He pushed away a bit and continued to stare at her, his arms on her forearms. Finally, after what felt like a short-long time, he nodded.

"You were waiting for some sign that things had started happening," Max said to Quinn.

"Oh, this is totally that sign," Quinn agreed.

"Right. So here's what we're going to do," Max said. "We've

been trained for field action, and we're going to fall back on that training. People down here are hurt, and Rune needs our help. Tell us everything, Anna."

It took the better of fifteen minutes and a lot of excited arm gestures, mainly because Max wanted to know everything that had happened since the coronation gala. After she finally paused for breath, Anna said, "Did we mess up waiting this long? Should we be finding this boudoir? It's way past eleven minutes."

"Domino chains," Quinn sighed. There was a hurt look on his face—*or maybe not hurt?*

"He was talking about a starting point," Quinn explained. "I don't think anything we do matters anymore. Our endgame is on rails."

"How do you know?" Anna said.

"Because the Fool is a Quinn," Max said. "I'll finish our part of the story on the way. This mansion isn't as safe as the one we're staying in—let's get back to our room."

As they made their way through the bizarre setting of an old, tattered mansion tilted at a forty-five-degree angle, Max talked about the Eidolon, Lady Time, Quinn's drugged state, the other principalities, Lord Fool's familiar type of prophecy...

"Isn't that strange?" she asked. "Having three principalities no one knows about? I thought there weren't many of them."

Max gave her a quick head tilt, his way of smiling at her.

"Fine," Anna said. "I thought there weren't many of *me*."

"That's what I thought too," Max said. "Rune needs to hear all of this. But first, we need to find out whatever secret Lady Time is keeping. Some sort of machinery, we think? If the Fool says we need to start in Lady Time's quarters, we'll go there as soon as we're ready."

"There's the window we climbed in," Quinn added. "It goes to the cavern outside our guest room."

Max told Quinn to go first, then Anna second.

Anna couldn't climb and aim her Slate light. "Can you make a light cantrip while I'm climbing?" she asked, and hid her embarrassed flush. "My concentration isn't as good as I thought."

"We can't," Max said. "We tried. Jerica—Fiddler Blue—said there isn't much magic down here. Your concentration is more than good." He leaned out the window and said. "Aim the Slate light up here!"

In the wobbly beam Quinn aimed at her, she climbed out a window and into a stone cavern, which was just as weird as it sounded. There *was* magic around them—she could sense protective wards in the cavern. Max had said that one of the principalities, Jerica, had made sure it was a safe place. But the normal, deep pool of magic she'd always felt on the streets of New Atlantis was thinner here, like mountaintop air.

The first thing they did inside their guest room—a sort of weird, converted solarium, like the one Rune held court in at Sun Estate—was open the trash bag Anna had stuffed the quickly-grabbed items inside. She pulled out the knife first and, with a show of great reluctance, gave it to Max.

"You have one of Brand's obsidian knives?" Max asked in surprise, which Anna pretended not to hear as she pulled out three tranquilizer darts.

"Do you have a dart gun too?" Quinn asked.

"No," she said. "I can't pick that lock. So you'll need to, you know, use these manually." She wasn't sure her peaceful friend understood, so she added, "Like, stab people," while mimicking an overhand stabbing gesture.

Max said, "You've been spending an awful lot of time with Brand. Is that why he gave you one of his best knives?"

Anna sighed. "Not really? He caught me in the weapon room last week while I was borrowing it. I told him I was hiding there because a girl at school said I had fat thighs. He went back outside and texted Corinne, and waited for her. I nearly had time to pocket a grenade!"

She pulled out the cash and said, "Will this help?"

"That'd buy a lot of ivory soap," Quinn said. "Nice one, Anna. Is that my sigil belt in there?"

"I think so? But it only had—oops." She turned the bag upside down and shook it. The three platinum discs had been knocked loose from the leather holster. "Shoot."

"Oh, that's my kid belt," Quinn said. "I don't use that one anymore. Do you remember which side of the belt the sigils were on? I've got this limerick, you know. *Lots of defensive stuff on the left, really bad stuff on the right.*"

"How is that a limerick?" Anna said. "You don't know what spells are in there?"

"I can tell that there *is* a spell inside them. And it's probably either Telekinesis, Shield, or Healing. I always had a backup of those. Oh! Is that Queenie's snack mix?" He snatched the plastic bag greedily.

"You had Queenie make you a snack?" Max asked. "Does she know we're here?"

"No and *no*," Anna said. "I can make my own snacks. She just saw me going outside and offered."

Max adjusted the weight of the knife in his hand, satisfied. "This is really good, Anna. I think we need to move out. Quinn, do you want the sigils?"

Quinn put the sigils on the left side and fastened the belt. It was tight around his waist, but he could secure it on the last notch. "Ready."

Climbing up the dumbwaiter shaft wasn't as bad as Anna feared. All of those upper body exercises Brand made them do were paying off.

Max, who'd gone first, hauled her through the upper floor opening. "Lady Time's quarters aren't too far away. We've only been in a dining room and some sort of courtroom, but her living quarters should be nearby."

As they walked the corridors—now sloping upwards, but

with an angle not nearly as bad as the mansion Anna had been portaled into—Quinn said, "I wonder how much trouble we'll be in."

"You didn't wonder about that until now?" Anna said.

"I wasn't exactly sure I'd have a Now," Quinn answered.

Max's face went tight at that, making Anna suspect he hadn't told her *everything*. She said, "Addam still talks about that time you ran away to get a papaya."

"That's not fair!" Quinn protested. "Someday he'll admit he overreacted. If you forget that an international portal was involved, even Addam would say that I was old enough to walk up to a market stall and buy merchandise politely."

"The way you see the world," Max muttered. "Stay here for a second—the rooms are down the next corridor. I want to scout it. Anna, teach Quinn the hand signal for *wait-in-place*."

"He's just kidding," Quinn whispered to Anna.

"No he's not, you're awful at them," Anna said.

"Sometimes I remember different hand signals that Brand *might* have used. It's hard to sort through all the possibilities because his most popular hand signal isn't really an instruction. Not that it matters anymore; I don't see any possibilities anymore."

"You don't know if that potion will last forever," Anna said. "Max said that Corny-whatever told you that."

"He also said it *might*. But that's good, right? I'm one less special person everyone needs to protect."

Anna showed him a flat hand, and pointed to the spot where he stood. Then she said, "Are you serious?"

"…Yes?"

"You honestly think you're suddenly, magically unimportant? The kid who saw all our futures? Is your hand broken?"

"My hand?"

Max came back. "Clear. I don't even see the guards outside the room. What's wrong?"

"Nothing," Quinn said, as Anna said, "Quinn doesn't

think he's important anymore because he can't keep seeing the future he's already seen."

As Quinn gave Anna a look she dismissed as "short-term betrayal," Max bristled and expanded two sizes, just like Brand did when someone said something stupid.

"Are you kidding me?" Max said. "Do you have any idea how much harder you're going to have to work? All of the answers are in your head and you can remember them. You have got to write that shit down and interpret it. You can't rely on your gift to give you the answers—it will take *work*. You are so damn important. You've always been our advance notice and that has not changed. Unless you have amnesia? Unless your hand is broken and you forgot how to write?"

"I joked about the hand already," Anna said. "And you're also the only one with sigils. Plus," she added, and pulled the wad of hundreds out of her pocket. She poked it into Quinn's chest. "You should hold onto this. This is Addam's superpower, and you've spent your life around him. It's probably rubbed off."

"It really *is* one of his superpowers," Quinn said, and took the money. "You said there're no guards ahead?"

"Quinn, I swear to gods, we're going to talk more about this later," Max said, but he also let the matter drop.

They quickly crossed down the last mansion hallway to a heavy door. On the other side was a room that smelled like old food and fresh fruit. A comically overdone red velvet chair— the only comfortable seat in the room—was set against one wall.

"The Fool said the boudoir," Anna pointed out.

Max nodded. "We should go there first. I don't think we have time to do a real search."

Real searches, Anna had been taught, weren't easy. It involved a lot of unscrewing, lifting, and lock smashing. She was perfectly happy speeding through a series of chambers on the gas of Lord Fool's prophecy: past this courtroom, through a dining room, into an antechamber piled with new gowns lazily discarded on furniture. There was only one room with a bed after that, so they stopped there.

"What do we look for?" Quinn asked.

"Fingernail marks inside tight, locked spaces?" Anna muttered. "This is creepy."

"Look for anything in writing," Max said. "Anything that doesn't belong. Anything that tells why she has Revelry members march topside."

Anna ran through everything the Fool had said. One of his phrases caught her attention. "I think he said we start here. Maybe he saw a clue that leads us to wherever we need to go? I haven't seen any sort of machinery. We could... what is this?"

She'd found a small wicker basket containing sigils. They were just tossed there like costume jewelry, buzzing with potential. The one on top was a diamond... thimble? But there were stainless steel pins on it?

Quinn peered at it, confused. So did Max, until insight flashed and he quickly turned his skin pearlescent to hide a blush. "I think," he said carefully. "It's not unlike, er, Rune's thigh sigil. But for a person's chest."

"Atlantis was weird," Anna muttered, and dropped the, for lack of a better term, nipple crown back into the basket.

Max found a stack of notes on a desk written in old Atlantean. Since he'd had the most training in it—his grandmother had once started teaching him the language, he said—he puzzled them out while Anna searched a closet.

"This mud," she said, pulling out a pair of ruined velvet slippers. "Wasn't there something about that in Rune's notes? I think he mentioned it again after the bunker meeting. This is why they suspected Lady Time might be in the Warrens, right?"

"It's definitely dirty around here. And I suppose it can get muddy when it rains. But I haven't seen a lot of mud that greenish color," Quinn added.

"This note talks about a library hallway," Max said, holding up a crumbled yellow post-it. "I think it says *left at the library hallway.* Something was left there? Or it's a direction to go left? Maybe something important is stored there. I bet there's a library in one of these mansions."

That was when the door to the room opened, and a short, stout woman with crimson hair leaned through the doorway. She was wearing a magenta raincoat that swept to her calves.

"Oh, you've got to be shitting me," she said. "What the hell is happening here?"

CHAPTER NINE
Anna

The woman, introduced as Jerica, was massaging her temple in frustration. Even after Anna explained that Lord Fool hadn't given her many options.

"This is not an adventure," she said. "It's not a game. You're in so far over your heads. Do you understand? Let me put it another way: this is the point in the horror story where smart kids grab each other and hide, not invite more people as cannon fodder."

"Where is the library?" Max interjected, waving his post-it. "We don't have time to argue."

"What library?" Jerica asked, distracted.

"It may be in a hallway. Is there any hallway with a bunch of books?"

Jerica froze. She reached a hand toward the post-it, and Max handed it to her after a second's pause. He said, "Do you know what this means?"

"I know what it could mean. The Eidolon has… a lot of strange parts. I don't think you appreciate how big it is, or how small our own area is."

"Do you know where Lord Fool is?" Anna asked. "Maybe he can tell us more. Someone has to know what Lady Time is hiding."

"I've lost track of the number of things Lady Time is hiding," Jerica dismissed. "She doesn't trust anyone. We all have pieces of information. How are you sure this secret is worth the effort of learning it?"

"Why would Lord Fool—who is a Quinn—" Anna said, while Quinn made a sound of protest at the new noun, "bring me here and point us in this direction?"

"Anna," Max said sharply. His skin went pearlescent again. In a very careful tone, he said, "we already guessed Lord Fool sent you so you could bring us sigils and weapons."

Rune seemed really, really, *really* determined not to let many people know she was a strong magic-user. Max probably wanted to hide the fact that Anna didn't just come with weapons and magic. She was the magic.

Jerica looked like she wanted to ask more questions about precisely that, but Max bludgeoned her with questions. "Do you know where the Fool is? Can you take us there? Did you know he was a prophet too? Why didn't Lady Time take *his* gift? Is he too strong for her?"

"He swore a vow not to work against her," Jerica said, chewing on her lip. "I was there."

"I've got some experience with Quinn Vows," Max said. "I bet he played around with the wording. Otherwise, how could he help us?"

"He could have made a vow to someone even stronger first," she murmured. Her indecision appeared to vanish. "Okay. The Fool has taken up residence on the edge of Lady Time's patrolled area. We'll need to go through the chalets. Let's try to avoid Maon and his guards. Maon isn't someone we want to bump into, not with Cornelius away on a mission."

"What is she planning up there?" Max asked. "Everyone is calling it a protest."

"Like I said," Jerica said. "The woman has secrets. I know her focus is on the Arcanum and Farstryke is her ancestral home—I just don't know how it all fits together. All of these people could be in danger. They'll need me close by."

"Then help us get to Lord Fool while you can," Max said. "Please."

"Follow me," she said.

They hurried through the bizarre collection of underground "McMansions" that Max and Quinn had mentioned. It seemed arrogant to name them after fast food, though. Even the main halls of these small mansions were bigger than the entire second floor of her last house.

They moved from function to function—storage, dining, even a greenhouse mansion filled with grow lights and generator fumes. One of the mansions they passed appeared to be filled with wood-and-wire rabbit hutches.

Quinn said, "It's called the murder—" and Max shushed him. Quinn quietly added, "It's called the MZ."

Anna looked at the rabbits through the doorway again. She also heard chickens and, possibly, a goat. "Does the Z stand for Zoo?"

Quinn looked at Max sheepishly. Anna just stared at Max, mutely letting him know what she thought of this shushing business.

They kept walking. They climbed through holes hacked in walls and doors that opened from bedrooms to garages. "Is there really a pooping mansion?" Anna asked. "I don't get how it works. Are there extra toilets?"

"No toilets," Max sighed. "Big plastic sealable bins. Eventually, they barricade off one room and move to the next when it gets too full. It's a big celebration when that happens, we heard."

Anna spent the next few minutes deciding if she was glad she'd asked.

There were a lot of people-watching opportunities, too. The crowd was excited. Many of them were drinking something that smelled like onions. Others were cheerfully bartering for better boots, walking sticks, bottled water, or homemade weapons.

Anna angled her Slate wristwatch at some point and started recording. Carefully and sneakily. Rune told her that many Atlanteans—especially the older ones—always forgot how dangerous technology was. And Rune would know. He'd once pulled out his phone in front of the Hanged Man, and straight-up called for help without the Hanged Man realizing it.

"This is where it gets strange," Jerica said. She opened a door from a mansion filled with musical instruments and comic books. On the other side was a bare cement cellar, and a hole was dug through the middle. "There's an entire complex of chalets beneath us. Don't think of the Eidolon like the surface—there's no floor. It spins out in all sorts of directions, including up and down."

"Chalets?" Max asked.

"From the French Savoy region. An avalanche in the Alps destroyed a neighborhood filled with vacation rentals decades ago."

They climbed through the hole, its edges chipped by power tools. Beneath them was a small wooden floor with a pointed ceiling—a loft with sleeping bags on the ground and a ladder to the floor below.

"All the chalets are the same. Three floors. You lot go down to the first floor and stay there. Don't wander more than a chalet in any direction, and don't go into the upside-down chalets unless you know the route is safe. I've got to grab a guy's ear."

"You said we should watch out for Maon," Max reminded.

"And you should—but if he's here, he'll be further in, near where Lord Fool cooks."

Cooks? Quinn mouthed to Anna.

"He said something about French fries," Anna whispered back.

Jerica laid a hand on her belly. "He does make amazing fries. Now I'm hungry. Okay—go! I'll be back in a few minutes."

"Where are you going?" Max asked.

"I told you I'd look into the missing people. This is me doing that. Five minutes."

She climbed down the ladder ahead of them, pointed to a second stairway that led to the first floor, and vanished through another door that she closed behind her.

The chalet was more crowded than Anna would have expected. People were engaged in the same sort of merriment and movement she'd seen in the little mansions. And lots of drinking. There were rolled-up sleeping bags everywhere.

"You know we can't mention that you're a principality?" Max whispered anxiously.

"*Yes,*" Anna said on an exhale.

"Rune is really, really serious about that," Max said.

"Do you know what else Rune is serious about?" Anna asked. "Everything. Right up until the moment he changes his mind. Usually in the middle of something big, when no one has any notice. Have you heard the stories that Brand tells? He writes them all down in a list."

"Anna," Max said quietly.

"I know, I know, I'm a big secret. What are they drinking? It smells," she said.

"They make liquor from mushrooms and onions. It's a fae recipe," Max said, maybe a little obnoxiously. He picked up the pace so he could be the first down the second stairway to the first floor.

"We just learned that ourselves," Quinn whispered. "We're learning a lot today. I'm pretty sure I know what rabbit tastes like now, too. It's been really weir—"

The *d* hung in the air as they reached the first floor. Doors on either side of the widest level of the triangular chalet were thrown open, and what they saw was bewildering.

It looked like the next building was a basement? Or an attic? At least, it was as small as the attic loft they'd climbed into. The walls narrowed to a point *beneath* the planks stretched across it. Anna could see exposed wiring and puffy-pink insulation on the floor.

"She said to stay out of the upside-down chalets," Quinn said.

Nearby, a young man paused while stuffing snack bags of pretzels into a duffel bag. He smiled and said, "The next few upside-down chalets are safe, but don't climb up through them. They get less stable as it goes on, so be sure to use the ropeways."

"That chalet is upside down," Max clarified, and pointed.

"Every other chalet is. They're stacked like gears." He zipped his backpack shut and headed for the stairway.

"This is chaos," Max whispered. "Did the translocations fail, or break up during the teleportation?"

"It's not chaos," Quinn said. "Not at all. Chaos isn't this neat."

Since the young man had said the path was safe, they walked over the boards in the upside-down chalet. The next right-side-up chalet was identical: busy, excited, celebrating people.

"Let's ask around," Max murmured. "Try to figure out where they're going. Stay in eyesight of each other. Understood?"

One of Brand's top rules in the field was that there must always be a clear chain of command. Max was almost always the field leader in practice—and Anna had no desire to fight for *that* armband. So she just nodded and stuck close to Quinn while Max wandered up to the second floor.

It was only when she was on her own that she realized *asking around* was a lot like mingling, and she was not a mingler. Worse, everyone else seemed to know each other or be in a hurry.

She accidentally bumped into a girl her own age, who dropped an armload of water bottles. One of them cracked and splashed water, which made the girl shout *The Fuck!* at Anna.

In a second of instinct, her eyes began to glow a pale, pale amber.

"Holy shit," the girl said. "Nice. Bad ass."

Anna blinked, surprised.

"You with the nobles?" the girl asked.

"Um. Sort of?"

That was when Quinn swooped in with hundred-dollar

bills clenched in his hand. He said, "I'll give you this if you tell us where you're going."

All of the money. At once! Like he'd never heard about budgeting.

The girl took the cash with a glowing, ecstatic shrug. "Sure. Farstryke. We're demanding that the Arcanum lets Lady Time take back her castle. She's going to let us *stay* there. There are paths there from the Eidolon and everything."

"Good grief," Quinn said. "Do you know how haunted it is?"

The girl looked confused. She shook her head adamantly while gathering the unbroken water bottles. "Nah. They're keeping it from her. That's all a lie."

"The Arcanum is keeping it from her?" Anna said, which did not sound like anything she'd heard—or, fine, *overheard*— from Rune.

"Yeah. So we're going to the streets to demand it back. Nice meeting you, though. You're not that bad."

As the girl ran off, laughing at some people climbing the stairs above them, Quinn and Anna stared at each other.

"Does that sound right?" Anna asked.

"No. Why is Lady Time making a spectacle over Farstryke Castle?"

Quinn *hmmmm*'d himself into a fit of thinking, leaving Anna in her brain, turning over what she'd learned. She didn't know the answer—but she knew Quinn had asked a very good question. He was really smart about figuring out why people did what they did.

Max tramped down the stairs and joined them. "I heard. Farstryke? They want to move into Farstryke? That's weird."

"I don't think…" Quinn chewed on his lip. Then he shook his head, clearing his thoughts. "Well, really, I don't think that's our mission. It's still info Rune needs, though."

They heard Jerica's strident voice in the next chalet, greeting and talking to people as she made her way back to them. There was a smile on her face as she entered the second chalet, but it dropped away as soon as the four were huddled in a group.

"You're right," she said, clearly upset. "People are missing, and not just the sort of people who'd wander away on their own. We need to find Lord Fool."

She led them across more planks in an upside-down chalet, then up the stairs and loft-ladder of a right-side-up chalet. In the pointed attic of that building, a door opened to a thick twine rope bridge, strung from wall to wall. Jerica advised, "You can't trust these floors. Or ceilings, really. Some of them have collapsed completely. Hold tight to the rope just in case."

The reason for her advice soon became obvious. By the time they'd passed through three upside-down chalets, the crowds in the right-side-up chalets thinned, and they reached overturned buildings where every floor had crumbled or cracked into a distant heap below them. The thick rope guide was replaced by a rope bridge. As they crossed the unstable path, their flashlight beams picked up the leftover bits of unplanned abandonment far below—ski poles, mittens, a bright throw blanket, a pet's red plastic dish.

The deeper they went into the complex, the more signs they saw of avalanche damage. It was also darker, without the lanterns and flashlights of residents.

Anna summoned a light cantrip—automatically pumping more willpower into it, trying to push through the sluggish trickle of magic around her. The sudden brightness was so dramatic that it was almost a popping sound.

Jerica stopped dead in her tracks and stared at the grapefruit-sized ball of white light. "Hmm," she said faintly. "Not everyone figures that out."

Anna felt the heat of shame rising under her collar. *Stupid stupid stupid stupid—*

"She practices a lot," Max said immediately, "She's the best student Rune has ever had."

"Of course," Jerica said, and let it drop. But Anna felt Jerica's eyes on the back of her neck.

Then Max put a quick hand on her arm, and shared a smile with her. The anger inside Anna sizzled away like steam, laying bare her genuine worry that she'd messed up. And then that sizzled away too, because Max was looking out for her, and he wasn't mad, even if he had a right to be. Max wasn't so bad.

"By the way," he added, raising his voice. "Are we ignoring the man perched above our head?"

There was a lot of quick, surprised shuffling. Anna's cantrip shot upwards, followed by Quinn's Slate flashlight. Perched on an old TV mounting was a man in jeans, cowboy boots, and a dirty white shirt.

"Jerica," the man said coolly.

"Juror Waylan," she said back, and seemed relieved, despite the chilly reception. "We need to talk."

CHAPTER TEN
Anna

"Do you know who he is?" Anna managed to whisper to Max while they followed this Juror into a right-side-up chalet. There were no more crowds by this point, or even stragglers. Anna saw only a few beds and no sleeping bags.

"I think Quinn does. Or, you know, *does*," Max said, and wiggled his fingers next to his head.

The kitchen on the first floor looked like an actual kitchen—with a small stock of food and a hot plate. Juror dropped heavily into an armchair while flicking his hand at other chairs and a sofa that sagged so low in the middle that it touched the ground.

"I heard we had guests," he said in a deep voice.

He had dark skin and a raw, compelling face—the sort of face you'd want to call beautiful or handsome, but not both. On his arm was an Arcana seal. A real Arcana seal.

"Juror is Lord Fool's seneschal," Jerica said.

"Was," Juror said, and dropped his eyes. "No one following me now."

He began to pull off a boot. He wore no sock on his left foot; just old white medical tape that had dried blood spots. Juror picked up a fresh roll of wrapping from a table near his chair and began to replace the bandage.

"I'm glad they released you," Quinn said. "I know the charges were false. You were a really good representative in the

Convocation."

Anna began to remember a little of that. Some sort of scandal? A young representative stepped down? And, apparently, made his way to the Revelry...?

"Green mud," Max said suddenly. When eyes snapped toward him, he pointed at the boots. "You have green mud on your boots."

"I do," Juror said, but thoughtfully. "And that means something to you because?"

Max looked at Quinn, looked at Anna, then seemed to make a decision. "It's one of the few things the Arcanum knows about her. It's why they're searching the Warrens."

Whatever that meant to Juror, he kept to himself. He continued to stare at Max.

"Juror, do you know people are missing?" Jerica said.

His gaze snapped back to her. "What do you mean?"

"Not wandered off. Not returned to the surface. People who you wouldn't expect to go missing have vanished. I've heard an unofficial count of twenty-six missing members of the Revelry."

Juror stopped moving, frozen in the act of putting his boot back on. Then he lowered his eyes, pulled the boot on, and tapped the heel into place.

"Her backhand was inevitable," he finally said. "I told them. I fucking told them."

"Why go after the Revelry?" Max asked. "Why not another court?"

"Why not? We're a ready force with loose leadership. It's the nature of the Revelry. And the Fool is..."

"The Fool is a very, very strong seer," Quinn said quietly. "We know that now. And we also know Lady Time doesn't like seers working against her."

Juror stood up, surprised. "You met him?"

"He brought me here," Anna said. "He thinks we can help. I don't know why he doesn't help himself, though."

"She tried to neuter him with potions, but they didn't last.

He's had his gift for centuries—it's not easily stripped from him. But she did get him to swear fealty. I thought his hands were tied, but if he brought you here…" Juror looked down at his boot heels. "The mud is from another section of the Eidolon. Lord Fool knows… shortcuts. He's had me looking and searching, too. He suspects something is off."

"Have you seen any equipment or machinery?" Max asked.

"No. No," he repeated, shaking his head.

"Have you searched all of the Maze?" Jerica asked. "They found a note—a brief note—that may be a direction to a library hallway."

"Not all of it. The bears and bloodworms are a problem, and I don't have sigils to defend myself."

"Could Lord Fool know a shortcut there?" Anna asked, which must have been a good question because Max nodded along with it.

"If one exists, he'll know," Juror said. "But even with directions, it's a dangerous place to go. If he gives you instructions, follow them *precisely*."

"Gods, this place is insane," Max said.

Juror smiled at that—a crooked line on his serious face. "A lot of things look crazy until you know the whole story."

"There really are bears?" Max said.

"They aren't quite bears anymore," Juror said. "They cross between Warrens and Lowlands, and things that go into the Lowlands don't always come back the same. If any cross your path, put them down."

"Have you seen Maon and his crew?" Jerica asked. "We don't want to bump into them, either."

"No. I thought they'd be marching topside."

"Why is Maon so much trouble?" Max asked.

"He's a battle alchemist," Juror said. "If he throws anything at you, treat it like a blast radius. Maon and Cornelius are underhanded liars. I'm almost positive that Cornelius created the Agonies. We should—"

Jerica yelped. She rolled up her sleeve. A burn mark, in the shape of fingerprints, appeared around her wrist. The skin quickly paled and died, curling off her arm in large flakes. "I'm out of time. She's calling me topside. If I don't go, she'll send people after me."

"I can't go with you, either," Juror said. It appeared to frustrate him. "Lord Fool ordered me out of his sight. It's his way of protecting me."

"We have sigils," Max said, with only the faintest of pauses as he glanced at Anna. "I've got a good knife. We'll be alright."

"No, you won't, not unless Lord Fool tells you so," Juror said. "I'll take you to the cavern stairway—it leads to the restaurants, where he stays. Whatever he tells you, do it. If he says you can't go, don't go. If he tells you a path to take, take it. Do you understand?"

He looked at each of their faces, maybe until he was sure he hadn't wasted his breath. Then he stood up, said *come on*, and led them back upstairs and onto the next rope bridge.

When they reached the next right-side-up chalet, Juror climbed down the loft ladder and the stairway to the first floor.

He said, "The cavern stairway was our first big find. It was buried under a collapsed upside-down chalet. When we cleared the debris, we found the stairs and restaurants. The Fool seemed really excited about that. He's... his gift? What's happened to his followers? It's hurt him. Be nice to him, alright? He really isn't so bad."

Juror opened the door and showed them the basic frame of an upside-down chalet, but the ruined interior had been completely gutted and removed. The floor of it widened to a massive, spiral stone stairway with broad, shallow steps.

"Your name comes up a lot," Max said. "Around here. You've been holding them together, haven't you?"

Juror shrugged.

"We're trying to help you too," Quinn said.

"We'll take whatever help we can get. Go on now. Pay attention to whatever Lord Fool says—he buries a lot of real prophecy in what may seem like nonsense."

Anna very, very carefully did not glance at Quinn.

"Look after each other," Jerica added. "If I can come back, I will, but I can't disobey Lady Time directly."

Max took a deep breath and shared glances with Quinn and Anna.

"Let's go," he said.

"This isn't a translocation, is it?" Anna asked as they descended the winding stone stairway. She was lighting their way with her giant cantrip.

I've got to learn how to make that smaller, she thought.

"No. This was definitely carved with magic," Max said. He looked over at Quinn. "Are you ready to tell us why Juror is so important? You mention his name sometimes."

"Oh gods no," Quinn said. "One crisis at a time, Max."

"Are you going to write it down, at least?" Anna persisted.

"I probably should. But I don't think it's good to know some of that stuff in advance. I'll need to get a lock for the journal."

"You do that," Max said. "Anna totally won't pick it inside a day."

"I would never," Anna said, but crossed her fingers.

After five minutes, a light appeared before them—steady, unwavering electric light. The last revolution of steps had no rock walls—just an iron railing. It ended in the center of a cavern courtyard, not unlike the one outside Max and Quinn's guest room. Instead of being surrounded by mansions, they were surrounded by the glass storefronts of restaurants.

"I don't hear any generators," Max murmured. "But there's electricity."

"There's also an Arcana around here somewhere," Quinn pointed out. He frowned. "I think these are… American? I've seen pictures of these."

Anna walked over to one glass door. There was a sign on it listing hours of operation. She lightly ran her hand over the glass—not on it; she just skimmed the surface. It buzzed with magic. She reread the sign and said, "They're owned by someone called Howard Johnson. He liked orange. And there are some huge freaking worms inside this restaurant." She looked into the squirming shadows and swallowed the spit that filled her mouth. She saw Max pulling his knife from his belt and added, "But I think this restaurant is sealed. There's magic along the glass. We don't want to go through these wards—they're dangerous."

"That restaurant over there is lit up," Quinn said, and pointed to another storefront.

Anna counted five separate restaurants owned by this Howard Johnson. They looked very old—something from the years before she was born. Rune would probably know. He was always talking about the 1980s and 1990s as if they were the first decades of human existence.

They moved cautiously toward the brightly lit glass doors of that one restaurant. Anna ran a hand along the glass, but didn't feel anything more than protective magic. Nothing that would hurt them if they passed through it. She didn't have the vocabulary to explain *why* she knew that, but dangerous magic always felt hot-electric to her, not just buzzy-electric.

And then she saw the Fool—inside, moving from table to table, picking up wayward plates.

Max told the others to take a step back, and led them inside. A little bell above the door tinkled as they entered. Max immediately began to swipe his gaze from left to right, up and down. Anna hurried to do the same thing. Brand said the first thing you did in a potentially dangerous situation was to look for exits, ambush points, and tripping hazards.

Whoever used this restaurant were messy eaters. The Fool was looking at the food on the floor—actual chunks of food, not just crumbs—with a sad expression.

"I miss Ashley," he said quietly. "My dog. She loves table scraps."

He turned and walked through a swinging kitchen door.

The three looked at each other.

"We follow him, right?" Anna asked.

"Yes," Max said, but swallowed heavily.

They went past the swinging kitchen door, which smelled like lemon cleaner and showed the scuffs and permanent greasy fingerprints of many years. The kitchen on the other side was just as old. The appliances were larger than their modern cousins, and the countertops were in shades of orange and aqua. One glass cabinet filled with different kinds of oils had a padlock on it, and there was a dull mirror running along half the wall, which seemed really weird in a kitchen.

"I sent Francis to get more potatoes," the Fool said from his spot in front of a cutting board. "The guards like my fries, and it's a small way to keep them happy so they treat my old followers well."

"They still follow you, Lord Fool," Quinn said politely.

The Fool turned a sad look on Quinn. "Child," he said. "I know. That life is over." He looked down, shuffled over to a hulking fry machine, and fiddled with the knobs.

"You built the Eidolon," Quinn said. "Didn't you?"

The Fool hummed to himself for a few moments before replying.

He said, "I know you're scared of me. You'll be scared of me for a long time. Which is so silly. You have what I don't. Do you think your family would ever let you manage a fry machine alone?"

"No, and for so many reasons," Max whispered.

The Fool smiled, his mismatched pupils gleaming. "True story: there was once a group of humans who worshipped me. They turned their homes into elaborate magical mazes called ghost traps, to keep their wrongs from catching up with them. They're long gone, of course. Time erodes all mountains into riverbanks. But I always loved the practice, and I do have so many ghosts after me. The Atlantean War was... hard fought. We did so many things that will haunt us. I... I did..."

He shook his head with a tired sigh. "This place was built

with the help of the best prophets of a generation. They saw our needs for paths and pathways. I'm sure a path exists here just for you—but where will you go? Home? That's the safe choice. Or have you decided to meddle more? There's a path for that, too."

The Fool looked at each of them in turn. Anna found the one large pupil hard to avoid. It was like trying not to stare at an injury.

"We're meddling," Max said on their behalf. "Do you know the quickest way to get to a library hallway?"

The Fool hummed some more, then opened a cabinet filled with huge containers of spices. "The Maze of Hallways is miles away. At the very, very edge of the Lowlands."

"This Eidolon goes on for miles?" Anna said, thinking of the giant, toothy worms in the other restaurant.

"The Eidolon doesn't quite work the way reality works. Or maybe it does, but only if reality had strong mood swings." He reached up and massaged his forehead with a flour-stained hand. "It hurts, what you want to tell me. I don't think we have much time, children. It's all an angry blizzard ahead."

His head jerked up.

He whispered, "She comes. Hide. *Hide!* In here." He ran over to a door by the wall mirror. On the other side was an office—and the inside of the mirror was actually a window, too.

As soon as he'd shoved them into the office, he closed the door and raced back to the fry machine. His humming sounded forced—but Anna could hear the humming. Anna spotted a fine metal grate, like a speaker, to the right of the one-way mirror.

Several seconds later, a portal ripped into existence by the closed, walk-in freezer. Anna didn't have time to make out details about what lay on the other side before Lady Time stepped through and dismissed the magic.

Without a word, the three of them stepped close to each other. Anna felt Max's hand rest on her shoulder, and she also saw him reach up and touch Quinn.

"It's a glorious day, jester," Lady Time said. She walked a slow circle around the fry machine, staring at his bowed head.

"Look at that smile," Anna muttered. "It's like she just poisoned her stepdaughter's apple." And, okay, sure, maybe she stole that one from Corinne.

Max mouthed *shhhh*.

"You must See the path we're on by now," Lady Time said. "The Sun has been snared. Cornelius has removed him from the game board. The boulders are gone—only pebbles remain in my way."

Snared? Removed? Anna felt her heart start racing. Everything began to shimmer with an amber haze—and then Quinn's hand was painfully tight around her wrist. She saw his face, which was calm, and he held up a hand in the very correct signal for *wait*.

"Has he," was the only reply the Fool gave.

"He has. Strung them up on meat hooks, apparently. Sun and two of his muscular toys." She pulled a cigarette from a silver case, went over to a low counter piled with heads of lettuce, and leaned against it. As she lit the cigarette, she said, "I do not like this modern age much. There is no effort to it. It's bland and weak and uninspired. Then again, that weakness serves me, doesn't it? You must realize by now that my rule is certain. You will not be able to stand against me. No one will. Your followers? They are like cattle—they present no obstacle. The thugs that once ruled these underground hovels bow and serve me, and cut down my enemies. I have three principalities at my beck and call."

By this point, Anna had turned on her Slate and was recording Lady Time's helpful diatribe about how much everyone else sucked.

"Is there something you need from me?" Lord Fool asked, almost too quietly to hear.

"Yes. I want you to light a fire under the arses of your disarrayed court. I need *all* of them topside. Tell them to trust me and follow me."

Lord Fool raised his eyes slowly. Faint sounds filled the air around him.

"I'd think you'd be more worried at how close Lord Sun's children are to finding your secrets," he said. "They seemed quite interested in some sort of… machine?"

The cigarette dropped from Lady Time's fingers. She pushed away from the counter and strode over to Lord Fool. Then she grabbed the table filled with uncut potatoes and threw it across the kitchen.

Even Max jerked back.

"My path is clear," she yelled. "You dare taunt me? Tell me where your Francis is. I will turn his breastbone into *shackles* for you!" Her first backhand took the Fool across the face. He staggered against an unlit oven, cowering into his forearms.

"Would you like that?" Lady Time shouted. "To wear parts of your Companion as jewelry? You dare taunt me!"

Quinn pulled away from Max and Anna and went to the one-way mirror. He put both hands on the glass, screwed his eyes shut, and began to whisper words over and over and over. Anna heard him say, "And I will tell you about the harm she has brought to twenty-six of your followers, and I will tell you about the harm she has brought to twenty-six of your followers, and I will…"

Over and over and over, Quinn whispered this as Lady Time rained blows on the huddled Arcana.

The whispering Anna heard grew loud. The screams of ancient bedlam rode the air—the screams of madness and unchecked rage and bound wrists and jolts of electricity and cold water rising above your screaming lips.

Lord Fool straightened, and Lady Time took a quick step back from him.

"You think me toothless?" he said. "Even here? Amongst frayed wiring and spoiled chicken? Do you have any idea what I could do with that single potato peel by your left foot? With the burning oil in the vat before me? This room is a diorama of violence. The pentagram practically carves itself into the earth. Think very deeply on your next move."

"You know the power I can draw on," she said.

"I do not, but I'd love to learn more. If only you had time to tell me." He was standing straight by now, and there was no sign of the frail cook anymore. "But your Forerunner is dead—or soon will be. The Sun advances on their warehouse. Your plans unravel."

Shock paled Lady Time's face—for a moment. Only a moment. She recovered with a dismissive gesture that, possibly, shook a little. "No matter. What he finds in that warehouse will unman him. But that's an entirely different pantheon of enemy—and I suspect Cornelius and Vadik's other master will be very unhappy with them. Modern Arcana, for all their thin power, do seem to retain some of their bite in their tantrums. You will remain here. Promise me. Swear to me."

The Fool stared at her as the echoes of lost madness faded from the air.

"I will remain here so long as you rule," he said. "My vow, and my vow, and my vow again."

Lady Time, still shaken and furious, said, "This day will end with bloody hands, mark me. My gift may not be like yours, but I can see that much. And it will not be my blood."

"Not just," the Fool whispered.

She swiped a hand through the air, and another portal materialized behind her. This time Anna had a quick chance to see the scenery on the other side—some sort of dusty, cobwebbed wooden room. In the back of her mind, she wondered if Rune would train her on these portals that everyone seemed to summon without any sigils. Why didn't he use these all the time? He hated walking.

As soon as the portal faded, Max was out the office door. "Is it true?" he demanded. "Are Rune and Brand and Addam alright?"

"Oh yes," the Fool murmured. He stared at the spot where Lady Time had vanished. "Poor thing. She spends so much time manipulating threads that she thinks she's built the web we all play on."

They crowded close to the Fool. His robes were dirty, but he smelled like baking vanilla. He seemed unaware of the blood on his face from the beating he received.

Quinn said, somberly, "I promised myself that I'd tell you about your twenty-six missing followers the first chance I could."

"Yes," the Fool said, and massaged his temples. "You did. A very nice display of forced prophecy."

"We think they've been harmed," Max said, just as somberly. "I think... I think they've been harmed."

The Fool nodded, and didn't make eye contact. He waved an absent hand at Quinn's belt and said, "You've stood here too long. The leftiest one is Telekinesis, when you need it—but do hurry. They're hungry when they wake up."

"Wake what? Hurry where?" Anna blurted.

"Through the portal. I can only get you *near* the Hallways—and do not try this until you're older, dear," he said to Anna as an aside. "But close is good, because if I get you *too* close, you'll be early and won't get captured."

"Captured?" Max said.

"Exactly. It's about being in the right place at the right time. The rest is just story."

"About this captured thing?" Anna persisted.

"Not enough time. Listen closely. Find the secrets she keeps. Remember what you see. Tell others. There are those who will understand the importance. So, now, go west. West west west. Once you reach the Halls, take a left at the spot where Max has a fright, a right when Quinn's stomach growls, a left, a left again, and then like an arrow until Anna gets impatient. Then a final right."

He walked over to the office door, traced a quick, complex shape on it with his index finger, and opened it to reveal a taut, shimmery portal. On the other side was... Anna had no idea what that was. But the Fool was giving her a stern look, so she said, "Not until I'm older?"

"There's a dear," he said.

"Can I ask you a question?" Max said.

The Fool sighed, stared into the middle distance for a moment, then pointed back at Quinn's sigil belt. "The one on the right is Healing. No, no, child, not for me—you'll need it. And do save the middle one for Magnus."

"Magnus?" Anna said. "We're going to school?"

"Is that the question?" the Fool asked.

"No," Max said. "Are you saying we *want* to be captured?"

"There is no want. There is only swimming with or against the current."

"So we swim with it? That's the best possible ending?"

"You swim with it," he said, and that's all he said. He walked back over to his fry machine. Anna stood at an angle to him, and caught the quickest glimpse of grief on his face.

That life is over, he'd said.

Anna's last home had been in a rundown section of the city. Aunt Corinne had always said it was safer than most neighborhoods, because the people who lived there had once been important and had just fallen on hard times. It made sense, when you considered the haunted and sad looks on their lonely faces. Corbie had always been better at cheering those types of people up.

On impulse, Anna went to the Fool and gave him an awkward, quick hug. She whispered, "Thank you," and retreated before it became a Moment.

"I need a nap," the Fool said vaguely. "It's hard, keeping my thoughts in one place. Oh—it would be bad if Brother Sun learned of my involvement. Many timelines end if he gets angry with me before he needs help with the Anchorite. Perhaps a few small, white lies will be needed. Don't worry—someone will help you with those."

The open portal hummed with magic, and Lord Fool, sinking into a wordless fugue, occupied himself with picking the potatoes off the ground.

CHAPTER ELEVEN
Anna

None of them heard the portal close. They were all too engrossed in the enormous cavern around them.

It was the size of a battleship deck, filled with stairways and magic. *Filled* with stairways. Stairways that dead-ended, twisted like Mobius strips, ascended and descended a dozen times before seemingly bringing you back where you started. There were stairways carved into the rough rock walls, and stairways supported by nothing except magic. A small, thin waterfall filled one corner, from an underground stream or broken pipe. That entire corner sloshed with water.

And the *magic*, Anna thought. They might have been even further away from the surface, but magic suffused this area like hurricane winds.

When she was finally able to speak, she tried to pull her attention back to what had just happened. "I don't understand what Lord Fool said. Did you hear all that? Captured? Magnus? The *Anchorite?*"

"Plus what Lady Time said," Max said. "Do Cornelius and Vadik serve someone else?"

"She said they serve an Arcana," Anna said.

"Rune knows," Quinn sighed.

"Rune knows what?" Max demanded.

"That another Arcana had to have been involved in the fall of his father's court. He almost always knew. It doesn't make sense otherwise to him. I remember that. He just doesn't want people to know he knows."

Max took a few slow breaths. "That's not our mission. We need to follow Lord Fool's directions. West. Quickly."

Anna brought up a compass on her Slate. She still had no signal, but the compass seemed to work. She turned to face the wall to the right and said, "That's west."

"But which door? Or archway?" Max asked, because there were a series of archways along each ground floor wall.

"Let's check some of the corridors out on that wall," Quinn suggested. "Maybe we'll get lucky."

That made sense to Anna. If there were other exits on the west wall, they were above them, and hard to spot from their angle.

So they began to move at a jog across the dirty, natural cavern floor. The west wall had archways—nearly tunnel openings—spaced about fifty feet apart. Max, knife in hand, made the hand signal for cantrip light. Anna complied, sending her ball floating ahead of them, revealing a passage that ended in a sharp turn. Max, possibly overdoing it on the hand signals, made the *wait* gesture and slowly edged toward the turn.

"It's a dead-end," he called back.

They jogged down to the next archway, repeated the process, and found another short tunnel with a turn that ended in a solid wall.

"Ghost traps," Quinn said.

"Do you think the doorway is somewhere up there?" Anna asked, craning her neck. "Should we try to climb the stairs so we can see up there?"

"See if you can float a cantrip higher," Max said. "I'll check out the rest of the tunnels along the wall. Quinn, angle your Slate light for me."

While the boys headed toward the next tunnel, Anna followed at a slight distance, but walked in a wider arc toward the center of the room. She didn't need to try or even worry about trying; there was so much magic in the room that her cantrip sprang upwards with only a slight mental nudge.

The overlapping nest of stairways above her became brighter, even as the light pool around her dimmed. She tried to follow where the staircases led, but they were meant to confound. It reminded her of the mazes on the back of the cheap paper placemats at diners, which always shut Corbie up for a good fifteen minutes.

She heard something ahead of her: like road grit crunched under sneakers.

"What was that?" Anna said, only it was a whisper.

She looked over her shoulder. The light from Quinn's Slate was only a small round circle.

Heart pounding, Anna sent willpower toward her rising cantrip. The cantrip glowed brightly, stopped, and fell back toward her.

Thirty feet away, the dimness gave way to reveal a creature. Its unhealthy gray skin was stretched over a lean, muscular frame. It had four legs, and two eyes that flashed like mirrors. She'd never seen a bear without fur before, but she was almost positive that's what she was looking at.

It saw it had been spotted, rose on its hind legs, and snarled. Then it dropped back to the ground and charged her with near-silent thumps.

"Anna?" she heard Quinn say. Then, "Anna!" His Slate light began bobbing and growing as he ran back toward her.

Anna flicked a hand, and her cantrip swerved toward the bear. It stopped its charge long enough to swat six-inch claws at the ball of light. When its swipe passed harmlessly through the magic, it threw back its head and roared again, then dropped back into another loping charge.

A surge of Telekinesis surged across the cavern ground, kicking up dust. It made the bear shear to the side and nosedive into a skid.

The bear unscrambled itself, shook its head with an angry snuff, and snarled at Quinn. Another push of Telekinesis made its claws spark against the stone as it was shoved backward.

"Gods, it's resisting my magic," Quinn groaned. "I should be able to lift it!"

"The Fool said it wasn't like a normal bear," Anna cried back.

"Run for a stair—" Max started to yell, sprinting toward them.

Anna was staring straight at Max when another bear lunged from the shadows behind him, fastened its teeth around Max's lower leg, and yanked him off his feet.

Anna watched Max's pale face—his mouth open in an O of surprise—before he was dragged back into the darkness.

Quinn yelled, a sound of despair and fear. He ran after Max, crying out, "You run, Anna! You run!"

Max screamed from the darkness.

No.

No no no no no.

They hadn't been this brave and smart and come this far to end like this. Not Max. Not Max or Quinn. No to all of it—to being scared and weak and losing a family she'd just found. *NO!*

Something snaked through her mind—something large and real and filled with power.

Anna's Aspect exploded, drowning everything in an amber silhouette.

As the room filled with false daylight, she saw half a dozen more bears circling and flanking her. She saw Quinn trying to Telekinetically lift the bear attacking Max. She saw blood on Max's leg as the bear worried him back and forth like a rag doll.

NO.

As if she'd done it every day of her life—as if someone was telling her how to do it—she extended her senses, felt the receding swirl of Telekinesis that Quinn was wielding, and took it as her own.

She sliced an arm in a scythe sweep, and every bear in eyesight was thrown off its feet with graceless yelps, including the bear attacking Max. That one flew so far that it left the cone of light and splashed into the distant drainage water.

Max and Quinn were staring at her.

It didn't matter; there was no stopping; they still weren't safe.

Her eyes flared brighter with amber light—so intense that the boys covered their faces. She could sense the dissipating energy of Quinn's Telekinesis. The spell was nearly gone. Her magic reached for it again, and her power flowed along with the grasp.

All of them made sounds of surprise as they jerked into the air. Max and Quinn floated toward her as she floated toward them, and then they all rose like a fast-moving sunrise, amber light flooding outwards.

"Look!" Max gasped. He was pointing.

Instinct guided her. She couldn't see what he saw—couldn't see much through the bonfire of magic in her eyes. She just moved them in the direction he pointed.

She heard the sound of massive wings.

She heard cracks of thunder.

The last threads of Quinn's sigil spell ran dry. It didn't matter. Whatever had happened didn't depend on anything. Not the duration of a spell, not Anna, not anything. It was its own power, and it ate Anna from the inside out.

Seconds later, she almost twisted an ankle as they abruptly settled on stone.

The boys were saying her name and shaking her. They seemed worried about something. On her knees now, she dug her palms into her eyes and tried to rub away the afterimages, but the pressure in her head was still there, an aching, yawning need for magic. For *release*.

Anna realized she was crying. Almost sobbing. There was no way to describe what she felt. It was like those rare, rare moments when she remembered something about her father, and felt the grief of his death all over again. Only this wasn't grief—it was incomprehensible shock and inarticulate emotion.

"Anna, it's okay, it's okay," Max was saying.

"I can't," she gasped. "I can't stop crying. It's so much. It's so much." But her words were barely coherent.

Quinn nudged Max aside and knelt in front of Anna. He clamped both hands on her shoulders and stared hard into her eyes. Then he said, "I know you're there. Of all the times I knew you and remember you, you were at your strongest when you were a team."

His words made no sense—but the effect was thrilling. It was as if the weight of a whole other person lifted off her brain and stomped away in a huff.

She stopped crying and, embarrassed, wiped the tears from her cheeks. She stared at Max's bloody leg and said, "The Healing sigil."

"It's not that bad, save it," Max said. "I toughened my skin before it really dug in. I'll bind it for now." He gave his best friend a hard look. "Quinn, this better not be one of those times you can't tell me what's going on."

"I…" He trailed off, at a loss. "This shouldn't be happening yet. Anna is almost as bad as Rune. Why can't you both ever be *patient?*"

"What is happening to me?" she stammered.

"Quinn," Max said as he began wrapping his leg with a strip of torn pants hem. It might be the first time Anna had heard him genuinely snap at his best friend. "Is Anna being hurt?"

"No, no," Quinn said quickly. He looked at Anna again, only this time it felt like he was really looking at her. "I promise, Anna. It's… your Aspect. Your Aspect is special. It thinks. I promise it'll be alright. Have I ever lied to you?"

Anna continued to wipe her eyes for a moment while considering that. She finally said, "Can you really not see lottery numbers like you said you can't?"

Quinn smiled. "You sound better." He looked up at Max. "We should probably hurry. This is something for later."

"He didn't answer," Anna said as she grabbed Max's hand and got lifted to her feet.

"Welcome to just about every damn day," Max said.

"Did I catch fire?"

"Did you *what?*" Max said.

"Did I catch fire like Rune does? I felt bright."

"You were very bright. No fire, but…" Max looked doubtfully at Quinn. "It looked like something was forming above her head?"

"Her Aspect is growing," Quinn said again. He sighed. "Rune will be unhappy, but I'm not sure this is a secret we'll be able to keep much longer."

"What secret?" Anna said. She amended, *"Which* secret?"

"That you really are a principality of Atlantis," Quinn said. "It's getting more and more obvious."

To bide for time while she rearranged her face into something less disconcerted, Anna looked at her Slate and swiped back to the compass app. It pointed west, across the narrow balcony of stone they'd landed at the topmost level of the room. An archway was in front of them, wide enough to fit all three of them side-by-side.

Blatantly changing the subject, she said, "Did you see any other exits on the west wall? Is this it?"

"I think this is it," Max said. He was still dividing his upset look between Anna and Quinn. "Are you sure you're both okay to go on?"

Anna whispered the words for a fresh light cantrip and sent it into the tunnel. "Ready," she said.

The huge stairway room led to a series of equally strange translocations. They'd all have been bizarre enough in electric lighting, but they were fundamentally unnerving by cantrip.

They walked through a log meeting hall from a children's camp decorated with disintegrating construction paper flowers draped on the rafters. Crayon artwork had been hung on the wall like a museum gallery.

A swinging screen door on the west wall led to three offices. They reminded her of the welfare agencies she'd traipsed to with Corinne over the years. Lots of black, ropey lines and signs filled with confusing arrows pointing in all directions. The air was dusty, and her cantrip light made the floating particles flicker like stars.

In the final office, a giant red digital screen showed the number for who was next in line. Its cord hung limply and unattached, yet the numbers on the screen flashed to life as she passed, from nineteen to sixteen and back to nineteen.

"Are we even in... you know... our world?" Anna whispered.

"We're in the Westlands. Or below it," Quinn added. "I'm almost positive, just like Lord Fool said. Really, really close to the Lowlands. No one understands the Lowlands."

"Not even you?" Max asked. Pointedly.

"It used to hurt my brain to overthink it," Quinn admitted. "There are things in the Lowlands that prefer it that way."

This time, Anna caught the minuscule hesitation before he said *things*. She might be getting better at speaking Quinn. She checked Max's face quickly to see if he'd picked up on it, and sure enough, Max was peering hard at Quinn.

The third office ended in a glass door that swung open into an indoor tennis court. They had to cross the cracked floor in the direction of a cement ramp. Every now and then a tennis ball bounced or rolled toward the net, but never from a direction that any of them were facing.

By that point, Anna only had about a million questions about how ghost traps worked.

The downward-sloping cement ramp led to a town hall that had been snapped into pieces resembling, not unexpectedly, a maze.

It almost looked normal: a government building ripped out of small-town America, then dropped onto New Atlantis with a translocated thud.

But this was the Fool's ghost trap, so the final product had an extra glaze of bizarre. That meant all the hallways had been broken apart, the rooms discarded, and the corridors laid out in a disjointed, inconstant maze.

Short of the jagged, splintered edges of each turn—which revealed island dirt and bedrock—it was easy to fool herself into thinking the maze was an average administrative building.

"So do we really need to just keep walking forward until Max admits he's scared?" Anna asked. This hallway was filled with corkboards and official-looking notices. The overhead fluorescent lights were on, but the light that came from them wasn't artificial. It felt like actual sunlight.

"Until Max *has a fright*," Max said firmly. "That means a jump scare."

"You know, it's really frustrating when prophets forget to add better specifics," Quinn sighed. He said it with such borderline irritability and cluelessness that Max elbowed Anna before she could open her mouth.

"Let's just walk until we get to a left turn," Max said. "Lord Fool was trying to tell us the best way to get to the library. Maybe there's a library inside this building?"

There was a log on the ground, which turned out not to be a log at all. Just shy of kicking it out of his way, Max seemed to realize it was a stiff, giant worm. It was dead, but none of them knew it at first.

"Are you scared?" Anna asked, her heart pounding a mile a minute. "Did you just have a fright?"

"I see a left up ahead," Quinn said excitedly.

"I haven't forgotten you, you stupid first-act gun," Max murmured to the dead bloodworm. He kicked it out of their path, tightened his hand on his knife, and let Anna and Quinn walk ahead so that he could guard the rear.

The opening on the left was another hallway. Not the same

hallway—and there was a pulverized gap of wood and stone at the joint. But it looked like it came from the same sort of small-town complex. This hallway was full of doors that opened up to rock walls and had signs like "Parks," "Sanitation," and "Community Events."

They passed two rights—each leading off into a type of hallway entirely unlike the one they stood in—staring at Quinn every time to see if his stomach growled. At the third right, he asked if gassiness counted, so they voted and took that right. It led to a cement hallway flanked by empty prison cells.

"You need to keep calm," Max said to Anna. "You look impatient. You can't be impatient at every turn."

"How can I control that?" Anna asked, because when she was scared, she got impatient, and that emotional armor suited her fine. "This place is crazy. Exactly how many ghosts did the Fool create during the war? Don't Arcana ever just try therapy?"

They took a left into a bathroom hallway, then left again into a dirtier hall with hard basement floors. Discarded office equipment was stacked out of the way. This was the longest hallway yet. Torches—lit torches—were fitted into standing brass stands, spaced far apart, with wells of darkness between them. The ceiling overhead was made from cheap panels that were torn, their insulation leaking grimy pink tufts.

"Straight until we get to the library?" Anna asked.

"Just tell us when you get impatient."

"Stop saying that. I'm impatient because it's the final turn, so maybe we just look for books?"

That was when a bloodworm dropped from a hole above her head and landed on her arm.

She had a second to scream before it slithered into a coil, and a mouth and throat lined with teeth bit into her bicep—her entire bicep.

Max didn't hesitate. As Anna and Quinn smothered the flames on her sweatshirt sleeve, he grabbed one of the torches from its holder and laid the flaming end against the thickest part of the worm. The worm shriveled from the touch, hit the ground, and curled into a tight ball the shape of a giant coconut.

Max beat it with the torch again and again until the creature seemed to deflate into a limp strand. He said, "Screw you, Chekhov," while Quinn tapped his Healing sigil. He touched Anna's bleeding arm, and the deep toothmarks smoldered into barely-healed ridges.

"Jerica said they hate fire," Max said, and then paused when Quinn demanded a second to Heal Max's leg, too. "Everyone grab a torch. Let's get past this hall, quick."

Quinn handed the first torch he grabbed to Anna, which is when she saw the torches weren't wood; they were bone. A long arm or leg bone, maybe, hollowed and smoothed and filled with sharp chemicals.

They took the rest of the basement hall at a fast walk. Anna saw shadows squirming within the many holes above them, but the fire kept the worms at bay.

"You're brave," Max said from behind her.

She looked over her shoulder, confused.

"You—" He cut himself off, unsure what he wanted to say.

"I what?" she said.

"You... I mean, fire. You were in a fire, and it..." He looked at her burnt sleeve, then at her face. The side with the burn marks.

Her hair was tucked comfortably behind her ear; normally she kept it draped over the burns. At some point, she'd stopped trying to hide it around her family.

Max added, "If that had happened to me, I'd be afraid of fire, I think."

"Anna," Quinn said, and there was laughter in his voice, "is not afraid of fire. But don't ask me about that."

Anna breathed through her nose for a second. Was this how Rune felt when Quinn made vague comments about how dangerous or surprising his life was about to be? "Just make sure you write it in your journal," she said, betting she'd be able to pick the lock with a paperclip.

Max said, "Guys. Look. Books."

The final hallway was a section of a library. The wooden shelves were neatly arranged, though cobwebs stretched between leather bindings.

"Shakespeare section," Quinn murmured and ran a finger along a book sticking out further than the rest. *Love's Labour's Won* was printed in gold along the spine.

"Guess it's too much to hope for the section on freaky metaphysical pocket dimensions," Max said.

"There's torchlight ahead. On the left," Anna said. Her own torch made a matted spider's web flare and shrivel, so she held it more carefully away from the yards of brittle paper. "I hope this is over."

"Are we getting captured next? I really wanted to know more about being captured," Max said.

They'd reached the turn. Instead of another maze hallway, there was a large, circular stone room. Parts of it were damp and covered in a thin layer of mud. The floor sloped to a grate in the middle. A stone slab as large as a full-sized mattress was set over it, braced on smaller stone legs. Runes were carved into the surface. They didn't glow, but the engraved edges of the chisel marks were colored a vapid green.

Next to the slab was a large handcart—the sort of thing department stores used to push large boxes and crates around. There were only two exits to the room, both reinforced wood-and-metal doors. One door was open, showing a room filled with scraps of fabric and bedsheets. The second door was closed.

Anna aimed her Slate at the table and began to photograph it. Wasn't this what Lord Fool said they should do? He didn't say they'd understand Lady Time's secret—he said they needed to find the secret and bring it to others. So she took photos, even close-ups of the runes, breaking the images up into sections.

Tucked under the slab was a smaller handcart. On this one was a selection of knives. Many kinds of knives—one as tiny as an ice pick, one as wide and serrated as a handsaw.

"Oh," Quinn whispered. "Oh no."

"What? What are you seeing?" Max said, which made Anna realize Quinn wasn't looking at the table like she was.

"The ward. On the door. I know what that is. Do you remember?"

Max blinked, surprised. "Remember what?"

Quinn walked to the closed door and stared at a round clay domestic ward. Anna walked with him and, when Quinn didn't object, feathered her fingers over the ward's surface. She couldn't identify the magic, but it was strong.

"I heard the staff at my mom's Westlands compound talk about it. Ashton Saint Gabriel put that on a door when he was trying to…" He implored Max with his eyes.

"Oh," Max said quietly.

"Guys," Anna said sharply. "What?"

Anna had the distinct impression Max was deciding whether to lie to her. She decided to give him a chance to do the right thing before making it clear what that thing was.

"Ashton used a ward like this to hide the smell of a body," Max finally said. "We need to look in this room. I think I know what we're going to find. Anna, it's your choice—it really is. But if you want my opinion? You don't need these images in your head. And I don't mean just because you're the youngest. No one should have to see what I think we're about to see."

Anna considered that. She really did. She didn't *want* to see bodies. She just wasn't sure whether she had a choice.

Struggling with the concept, she finally said, "Everyone says I'm going to be a principality or an Arcana. Right? I could be like Ciaran and not have a court to worry about, or I could be like Rune."

Quinn smiled. "Ciaran worries about plenty. Trust me."

Max said, "He once sat on me to keep me from running off alone. Ciaran is an acquired taste."

"Well, then, maybe that's my point, I guess," Anna said. "He'd do the same thing that Rune would. It doesn't matter what I am—I just need to be the kind of person with power who looks on the other side of that door."

Max flipped the dagger around in his hand and pounded the hilt against the ward. It took three tries before it cracked and fell.

The odor didn't seep out right away. Or at least, her brain seemed to fight acknowledging it—it flipped between smelling her own sweat and dirtiness, to the smell of...

She thought she'd be able to guess what death smelled like. She'd imagined it'd be like flattened animals on her old street before the city came by and scooped them up. But this was worse. It was personal. It smelled like full toilets and public restrooms.

Max and Quinn were blocking her view, so she finally put her hands between them and pried them apart.

Inside was a large walk-in closet. Rolls of carpet and plastic were stacked in the corner. That was her first thought.

Then she saw ankles and socks and bare feet protruding from the ends of the rolls. And through a wrapped log of plastic sheeting, she saw the blurry outline of a young face, as young as hers. One roll of bedsheets was loose enough to make out a set of sneakers. Pink hearts and roses had been drawn on the ratty canvas with pen ink.

Blinking back tears, Anna lifted a shaky arm and took photos of the room. Quinn followed her lead after a moment. When they were done, they all backed out of the room and closed the door.

Max looked like he thought he should say something; Quinn looked like he wanted to be sick; and Anna was blinking her eyes because she would not cry again today. Then Quinn took one of Max's hands and one of Anna's, so Anna and Max reached for each other at the same time, and the three just stood like that for a minute. No one spoke, and no one fell apart. They just needed that minute.

"I know," Max started, and had to clear his throat. "I know I should check the bodies. See if there are… wounds. Or what type of wounds. I just need a minute, though."

"She's really killing people," Anna said. Her voice shook as much as Quinn's arm. "And that equipment out there is involved. What is she getting from it?"

"Power," Max said. He glanced at Quinn, anticipating his nod. "Everything she's done, everything she's said—it all comes down to power. I just don't understand what *kind* of power you get from killing people. Is it necromancy?"

"We can ask Layne," Anna said. "Or Ciaran. Lord Fool said there would be other people who would understand what we saw. I took pictures of the table and all the runes on it."

"Quinn, can I borrow your Slate?" Max asked. "I'll check the bodies. You both keep an eye out. Anna, you might want to hide your Slate. We'll need to smuggle them out."

That's how the next five minutes went. Anna wasn't sure if it was awful or just anticlimactic, but Max went back into the room with the bodies to check for wounds while Anna and Quinn sat on the floor against a wall and waited to be captured.

They were all staring at the young fae as he finished what he probably thought was a stealthy entrance.

Standing at the archway to the maze was a pale, red-haired young man. A leather harness filled with tiny glass vials was strapped across his chest, and he held a metal rod in one hand.

"Maon," Max said. "The Fool told us to expect company."

"You'd think, by this point, you'd know when to ignore prophets," Maon said. "The Fool hasn't done you any favors."

"I'm curious," Max said, ignoring that. "How long did you work for the Heart Throne?"

"What makes you think I worked for them?"

"Because I haven't met an asshole faery in New Atlantis yet

who hadn't worked for them."

"How quickly you've turned on your own people," Maon tsked.

"I've got nothing against faeries, just what they became on this island. Why do you think mainland fae cut ties with us? My grandmother rotted us to the core." Max made a disgusted sound. "Let's be done with this. You have your orders. Take us back."

"My orders," Maon said, "were to subdue you first. I'm looking forward to that part."

He ran his fingers along indentations in the metal rod he held—three soft clicks—then pressed the rod's tip against his forearm. He exhaled a hiss through his gritted teeth.

"Battle alchemist," Max yelled, a second before Maon launched forward as a blur.

Maon hit them like a wrecking ball. Anna was thrown into the stone slab so hard that she flipped onto the surface of it. Quinn tumbled in another direction while Max was pinned under a rain of super-fast blows.

Anna scrambled off the table, let out a primal bellow, and charged Maon. She had this thought of tackling him like a punching bag and knocking him off Max, but Maon simply swung a super-powered arm into her stomach and sent her flying backward.

Max shouted in response and scratched Maon's face. Anna raised herself to a wheezing crouch in time to see Max's hand come away bloody with fingernails that curved into real, six-inch talons. Maon bunched his hand in Max's shirt and swung him up into the air like a rag doll. Max flew over the stone slab and crashed into a wall.

She felt the pressure of magic build in the back of her skull—and then squeezed her hands so tightly into fists that her nails burned little crescents into her palms.

There was enough magic floating here. She didn't need more. Didn't *want* more. It was enough to know that Maon was using alchemy to hurt her friends; and that alchemy was a type of drunkenness; and then to remember the tricks the adults in her life used to deal with drunkenness.

She whispered a sober-up cantrip, drew on the magic around her, and slammed every straining inch of her willpower into it.

Maon, stalking after Max's barely-moving body, jerked to a halt with a sound of surprise. He rubbed his fingers together and shook his arms, confused. Just before he thought to inject himself with more drugs, Max gave up the pretense of unconsciousness and rolled to a half-upright position while sweeping out a leg. Maon lost his footing and crashed to the ground. Max began to punch him in the face while Quinn ran forward and kicked the metal rod to the corner of the room.

"ENOUGH!" a man in green leather roared from the entrance to the chamber. Vadik—the principality.

Then he unleashed a wave of magical Telekinetic force that had all of them flying into the nearest wall, pinned to their tiptoes.

"You seem cranky," Max gasped.

Vadik walked over and studied Max through that reptilian hood. He pulled a knife from his belt and said, "You are feisty," while tapping the blade against Max's cheek to punctuate every word. The crisscross cuts turned wire-thin red, and blood began leaking down Max's lips and chin.

Vadik dispersed the Telekinetic spell with an airy wave while strolling toward the room with the bodies. He kicked at the broken ward on the ground. "This knowledge won't do you any good. No one understands her secrets very well, and even then, she keeps the list of people who've laid eyes on this table small. Terminally small."

Max gave Maon a bloody smile and said, "You're so fucking dead. Nothing ever works out well for henchmen who know too much."

"The bravado continues," Vadik sighed. He snapped his fingers at Maon. "Get them in a line and bind their hands." He handed Maon a silvery disc. "I'll take them through a portal.

You use that other portal to levitate the equipment to Farstryke's main hall. Meet me in the square just outside the estate gates when you're done—that's where she'll join us. Understood?"

Maon bowed his head like a proper asshat. Then he caught Anna's smirk and glowered at her.

"Try not to get eaten by ghosts," Vadik added. "Even with the defense wards we threw up, Farstryke is unwelcoming."

"We keep hearing about Farstryke," Max said. "Why does everyone think the Arcanum is keeping it from Lady Time? It's a haunted dump. I bet the Tower would buy her a welcome mat and everything. Why do we even need to be at this demonstration?"

"You'll be an additional deterrent should your master move against us," Vadik said.

He regarded them quietly through his hood. Then he brushed a finger across part of his outfit—or maybe over a sigil under the outfit.

The spell that broke free hit them like a lifetime's worth of concussions. Anna fell after Quinn, but a second before Max started fainting as well.

ENDGAME
Max

I t was like waking up in the middle of a stampede. Max's attention fractured under overlapping shouts, a crowd's unrest, a mad frenzy of movement. He took three deep breaths to center himself. Then he focused again.

He was on the ground. His hands were bound. They were in a dirty concrete square in front of a rusting iron fence. On the other side of the fence were children with bruised faces.

He sat up with a lurch.

No. Not children. Ghouls. Staring at them hungrily from behind the wards that encircled Farstryke Castle.

Max squirmed around to look behind him. Anna was starting to stir from whatever spell had hit them, too. Quinn was already struggling with his bonds.

Maon and Vadik stood between them and Lady Time—or as much as you can stand in front of someone glowing and floating above the crowd. She spoke to armed guards gathered on a city street in front of the square, but her words were so amplified that he barely understood the meaning. More blather about how evil everyone was except her.

Max lengthened his nails—and felt them slide from his nail beds, as wickedly sharp as when he'd attacked Maon by the stone table. Max had learned more than one new trick on this mission. Those weren't just long fingernails; they were literal *claws*.

He rolled over to Quinn, whispered *It's me*, and began

cutting through his friend's bonds.

"She's been speaking to the crowd. It's all stupid stuff—well, not stupid, but it's all lies," Quinn said quietly when their heads were close. "I don't know where the other Arcana are, but they can't be too far away."

"I'll untie Anna. Try to keep Vadik and Maon's attention off me?"

Max did a slow, fat roll to where Anna was lying. She jerked away from his touch, so he began whispering her name quietly. When she stilled, he picked away at her plastic zip ties with his claws.

"They took my knife," he said. "Can you see anything to cut me free?"

"The dart," she said. "I put one inside my sock band. Hold still." It took a series of punctures to weaken the binding enough that Max could snap free with Anna's help.

All three of them kept their hands behind their backs, lying supine. There was enough noise to allow them a low, urgent conversation. Most everyone was enraptured by Lady Time's rant, which flooded the street like concert speakers.

"We've got to get out of here so she can't use us against Rune," Max said. "Can we—"

An unnatural silence fell upon them. Not metaphor or uneasiness—an actual, muffled silence. Anna said, "She's put a shield around us. And above us. A *huge* shield. Like a dome. I can almost see it."

"How far does it go? Can we hide in a nearby building?" he whispered back. "Maybe we can duck into the crowd?"

"No," Quinn said, but not like he was talking to Max. Or not entirely. He gave them a panicked look. "Oh no. Look down the street. Those are all the Revelry members—they're pushing on the wall, but—"

"They're on the other side of the barrier," Anna finished. She saw what Max did: an entire block away, the Revelry members were gathered in a group. "She's locked us in with just her guards. But why did she lock the Revelry people out? That can't be good."

"I must admit," Lady Time said, only this was her normal voice. She'd floated closer to them without anyone noticing. "It's quite the unexpected pleasure, hearing how slow everyone is to understand things." She wafted toward them and settled on the lip of a dry fountain. "You were poking amongst my private possessions. If I thought you comprehended what you saw, I might just be upset."

"Was the Fool right?" Max asked, trying to distract her, or at least keep her attention off Anna and Quinn. "Is Cornelius dead?"

Nearby, Maon had moved closer, along with Vadik. In earshot now, Max saw Maon stiffen like an electrical current had run through him. Vadik, veiled in scaly leather, snapped his head toward Lady Time.

Lady Time's smile stopped looking like a smile. "That's of no consequence," she said quietly. "I was due to lose a pawn."

"Well, for what it's worth," Max said, "he seemed like a pretty good person to die."

She looked like she was about to retort, then her head snapped in another direction, toward where the Revelry members had gathered in those numbers one street away. Whatever she saw, it didn't make her happy.

Max didn't know what else to do but distract her, hoping Rune was out there, moving closer and closer. So he said, "What do you think the Fool will do when he knows why you killed his people?"

"More inconsequence," she snapped, but her eyes remained drilled on the street as if she'd felt an approaching danger. "He's not an idiot. He knows they're dead."

"Actually," Max corrected, "I said *why* you killed them. The other Arcana will be interested to hear about the power you get from it. I know Rune will."

He had no idea if what he said made sense. He was going on his gut instinct—that the table *had* to somehow relate to Lady Time growing more powerful.

Lady Time stepped off the fountain's rim and walked over to him. She kneeled, unafraid, close enough to brush the hair out of Max's eyes. Max kept his hands in the fake-bound position, fighting the urge to flinch.

She said, "You're lying. You know nothing."

"Don't I?" he said. "You leave us with a room full of dead bodies—whose blood has literally *dried* in their *veins*—and think we won't put two and two together?"

She continued to stare at him. There was a tiny pulse fluttering in her brow—some sort of undefined emotion. "That was unwise," she murmured. "Because now I believe you."

And then, again, her head whipped back toward the street. "Someone has breached," she told Vadik. "Prepare for attack."

Shit hit the fan.

From every direction, and all at once.

A guarda patrol car—amber and green lights jostling crazily as it swerved through the crowded main road—looked like it was about to jump a curb and charge the courtyard. Lady Time sent magic against it; and in the headlong collision, the car and its driver broke apart into rust and blood.

On the other side of the small square, a second car, somewhat obscured by smoke, drove over onto the sidewalk and crashed out of sight. And above them, there was a brittle cracking sound as frost spread along the apex of the domed Shield.

Lady Time's attention narrowed on that. She lifted both arms toward the sky, and Max felt a phenomenal flood of magic rocket upwards. Above their heads—above the dome— the sky began to churn in a circular pattern, like dirty water down a drain. Fat tongues of lightning spat down.

Lady Time paused long enough to glance down at Vadik. She said, "Change of plans. Kill all three of them. Now, and before they speak to any other." She flew back above them, looking for an approaching enemy.

Max's world got very small after that as adrenaline flooded

his veins.

Quinn was the quickest. He let out a bellow and charged Maon, who swung him into the rusted gate by the collar of his shirt. Max threw a handful of dirt at Vadik's mask's eyeholes; then jumped up and ran at Maon in a flying tackle before Maon could hurt Quinn. He landed on the battle alchemist's back and began to rain punches down on him.

Orange fire formed in Vadik's hand as he levitated. The scion pulled his arm to launch a fireball. Anna had climbed to her feet like she'd face him alone—and that, that, *that* was when Max's terror turned to radiant joy, because he saw him. He saw Rune. Max saw Rune not twenty feet away, garnet blade aflame, hand extended.

Vadik's arms locked at his side as Rune's spell hit him. He dropped to the ground.

At the same time, someone else managed to break the Shield. The dome shattered into magical static—and the summoned storm collapsed upon them like an overturned swimming pool filled with live electrical wires.

Lady Time may have spotted Rune, but before she could react, stone eagles shrieked from the sky to attack her. Some sort of gargoyle or golem?

Rune smiled grimly at that, then gave Vadik *all* his focus.

"Oh shit, give him room," Max said. He'd seen that smile on Rune's face—and this was not the Rune you stood near. Max grabbed Anna's hand and Quinn's sleeve and dragged them as far away from Vadik and Lady Time as he could.

Rune launched at Vadik, straddling him. His sabre blade dissolved to the hilt, which Rune ground into Vadik's eye. Before he could fire, something distracted him—something so surprising that he stiffened in shock. Vadik took advantage of that hesitation to vanish—gone in a blink.

Stone cracked, and the remains of the eight gargoyle eagles hit the pavement like meteor strikes. Max barely had time to push the three of them in another direction.

Lady Time regarded them, both Max and Rune, and

pushed her arms outward. A rolling wall of force exploded from her—

—and Max felt another spell grab him around the middle. He, Quinn, and Anna were pulled away from the square, grasped in Telekinesis, skimming just above the asphalt. They came to a rough, rolling halt at Diana Saint Nicholas's feet.

"Behind me," she said quickly.

A guard with a sword charged them. Without missing a beat, Diana reached out with Telekinesis again, ripped what appeared to be a second door off Rune's crashed Saturn, and frisbeed it across the road. The thug took it in the gut and flew backward through a candle store window.

"Run!" she yelled. "There—that bodega. Set up a perimeter inside!"

Quinn was being helped to his feet by Queenie—*Queenie?*—and Layne was there too, getting Anna off the road. All of them raced toward the store, which looked closed. Layne, their arm outstretched and bloody, did something that had the door slamming open.

They ran into the darkness.

Diana was the last in the corner store. By the time she entered, Max had already found the light bank. "Lights on or off?"

"They'll see our light cantrips anyway," Layne said.

"Lights on," Diana agreed. "I want people watching every window and door." A whitish-green ball of light appeared above her head. She ran a hand along three platinum sigil discs fitted into her leather belt. Light—faceted like a diamond—appeared as a hard glimmer around her hands, and then the Shields flowered along the walls of the corner store, a hazy shimmer to Max's eyes.

As soon as they had a basic barrier and light, Diana rushed from teenager to teenager to teenager. "You all need healing. Line up for—"

An explosion rocked the entire store. The glass walls imploded inward. If it hadn't been for Diana's shield capturing the shards in an invisible net, it would have hit them like a hail of gunfire.

"Farstryke Castle blew up!" Layne cried out. They'd been in the process of pulling a set of blinds down and peeking between the slats. "Holy shit, I think the Tower did it. He's near the fountain with—"

Layne's words cut off with a gasp. They mumbled, "With Rune," and put the blinds back in place. Then they gave Diana a horrified look, who immediately went to see for herself.

"What?" Max demanded. He ran around a display of sunflower seeds toward Layne. "Is Rune alright?"

Layne grudgingly gave him their space, but Max wasn't sure what had caught their attention. He saw blood, and there were lots of bodies, but—

The ground buckled beneath them as a scream—a mortal scream, godlike in strength—ripped through the battle sounds. The store floor shook back and forth, knocking Anna into shelves, and making Queenie and Quinn grab at each other for support. Max banged into a candy rack and overturned it.

And again. And again. Each scream was a howl of unaffected rage. Max covered his ears and dropped to his knees as the Powers outside the store hurled universes of magic at each other.

Somewhere outside, stone cracked apart. From his spot at the window, he watched a skyscraper on the other side of the street begin to buckle and slide earthwards under the force of *that scream.*

"Building coming down!" Max shouted.

That was as much time as they had. The glassless windows—covered by Shields and dented blinds—went opaque as a wall of dust and debris, as large as a city block, covered them.

"What the fuck was that?" Max whispered as Diana knelt by him.

Diana grabbed his shoulder for support. "Judgment is dead. I think Lord Tower destroyed Farstryke. The Time woman is furious."

"Where are the other Arcana?" Max said, while his brain blankly repeated the phrase. *Judgment is dead?* Lord Judgment was the leader of the Arcanum.

"Rune and Lord Tower are facing her now," Diana whispered grimly. "That's all I saw before dust covered the area."

Max couldn't see anything happening in that square before the gates of Farstryke. "Have you seen Brand and Addam?" he asked.

"They're right here! Running down the street!" Anna shouted excitedly from another window. "Look! Aunt Corrine is with them, and Lady Death!"

Max ran over to her and saw, through the shifting plumes of debris, that Addam was in the lead. The others were fighting a path through guards. The area around the courtyard, where Rune and Lady Time were, was still obscured.

Addam vanished into the clouds of dirt at a sprint, heading straight toward Rune.

Lady Justice found them first.

Diana lowered the Shields for her. Quinn's mother was wearing leather armor in different shades of white. Ceramic trauma plates, etched with feather and web motifs, covered her vital points. She wore dozens of sigils—the traditional Justice discs, a wire-thin crown, a pendant shaped like a balanced scale. There were fresh scorch marks along the breast of the armor.

As she stepped into the somewhat-trampled bodega, her eyes went first to Diana, skated to everyone else, and ended, firmly, on Quinn. She didn't say anything, but she gave him a slight, almost relieved nod.

"There are things you need to know," she said, addressing

everyone. "Lady Time has fled our arrival. Her guards are routed. There are mass casualties on the street. Lord Judgment has fallen, and Lord Hermit has assumed interregnum leadership of the Arcanum. And Addam and Lord Sun are among the missing."

Max watched her hand tighten on Quinn's shoulder. It was something to focus on, because Max refused to understand the words, or why Anna stepped against his side and seemed scared.

"Ciaran—who has apparently announced himself as Lord… Oh, bother that, that can wait," she interrupted. She ran a hand along her brow, leaving behind a dirt streak. "Ciaran and Lord Tower are tracking Lord Sun—Rune—and Addam. Rune's Companion is with them. We need to secure Lady Dawncreek immediately. All of you—we'll want to move all of you to a safe site."

She finally let go of Quinn's shoulder. Quinn had a shocked, chalky expression. Anna and Max moved over to him so that they were all together.

"Rune will be back with Addam," Max whispered. "You know that, right? Brand would know if something was really wrong."

"Rune has to be back. It's the only thing that makes sense. But…" Quinn shook his head and refused to say anything else.

Anna let out an abrupt cry of despair. She'd stooped low and came up empty-handed. "It's gone! My Slate is gone! It has all the photos."

"What photos?" Diana and Lady Justice both asked at once.

"Vadik found them," Quinn said in disgust. "When we were still unconscious in that square out there. He stomped on them. We lost everything."

"Are you sure?" Anna demanded. "They didn't find them until we were here?"

"What photos are you referring to?" Lady Justice asked, again, and this time planted herself in front of them.

"We recorded Lady Time acting like an asshole," Max said. "And we took pictures of this stone table—this equipment—that she had hidden. Quinn and—" He spun the sentence in another direction before he said *Lord Fool.* "Quinn and his prophecy said it was important."

"I set mine to sync!" Anna said excitedly. "The moment we hit a wireless signal, it should have been backed up. I just need my laptop."

"We'll get your laptop from Sun Estate before we find a safe house," Lady Justice said.

"A moment," someone said politely from the doorway.

"Lord Hermit," Lady Justice greeted, lowering her head respectfully.

Lord Hermit, dressed as always in a simple, hand-sewn brown cloak, looked right at Max and his friends. "How important?" he asked.

"She brought us here as insurance," Max said. "But when she realized we'd understood what the equipment was for, she told Vadik Amberson to kill us on the spot."

"Before we could talk with anyone," Anna added. "She didn't want us telling you this."

"So you know what you saw," Lord Hermit clarified.

"Not even slightly," Max admitted. "But there was a stone table inscribed with runes, and lots of knives, and dead bodies. I checked the wounds, too. The bodies didn't have any liquid blood left in them—it looked like they bled out, and whatever remained behind was dry. It was bizarre."

"Dry," Lord Hermit said. "As in, no blood left in the veins at all?"

"As in dried blood," Max said and tapped some of the dried streaks on his face. "The blood left inside the veins was hard and crumbling."

Lord Hermit didn't say anything for a few seconds. His head was cocked to the side, and he stared at the ground pensively.

"We should—" Lady Justice began.

"Get me those photos," he interrupted. "Now. Immediately. Where is your laptop?"

"At Sun Estate," Anna said. "Or—"

"Magnus Academy," Quinn finished. He glanced at Max and mouthed the word, *Fool*, but Max had already remembered that Lord Fool had made a comment about saving a sigil for Magnus.

Max said, "We have laptops in our dorm room. We don't even need to go that far—we can use a terminal in the front office."

"I could ask Lady Death to take you," he murmured. "She's been asking after the younglings."

"I will take my son there," Lady Justice said, her Russian accent sharpening. "Lady Death may join us."

Max expected a portal or maybe flight. Ghost steeds were too much to hope for. But Lady Justice, not unlike her middle son, had her own magic: She called for a town car.

Apparently, she had three limos circling the streets around her whenever she left the Crusader Throne compound. "Gods," Max muttered to Anna. "Imagine having so much money you can afford to be paranoid."

Lady Death was flying to the campus ahead of them. Queenie had remained behind, and would accept a ride to the Pac Bell to stay with Corbie. Layne stayed too—saying they'd meet up with Corinne, who apparently was okay but shaking off the effects of a mental attack along with Mayan, and would pass them news as soon as they had it. Max suspected Layne also wanted to find Ciaran, since there was apparently some news about him, too. So much was happening.

The streets around Farstryke were filled with battle damage and debris from the building collapse, so they jogged two blocks south until a town car could rendezvous with them. A city-wide *shelter-in-place* alert had gone out, clearing the streets. The driver began chewing the distance between them and Magnus at highway speeds.

The back of the luxury vehicle, with its stretched, O-shaped ring of seats, was large enough for all six. Diana had insisted she stay by Anna's side.

Everyone remained silent for the first few minutes, casting nervous looks out the window. Max had rarely been so shaken by a battle; it was almost hard to believe the world could still exist without earthquake-shaking and explosions. The deserted streets after all that damage were an equally unsettling sight.

He buried his fear in fidgeting and observing.

Lady Justice had taken a seat right next to Quinn, but hadn't said anything to him. She didn't even ask what he'd been through. Max thought this awkward silence might be a good time to air his grievances against Lady Justice.

But just as he opened his mouth, Lady Justice turned her head to stare at him.

Her magic swamped him. He'd heard about her infamous gaze—Rune had once said it was one of the most unsettling Aspects he'd ever seen. First, Max saw his grandmother's eyes, but it was from a specific time—after those days of hope, but before the years of disgust. Then her eyes looked like Brand's, the first time he allowed Max to pull a prank on him. But the eyes also looked like a barista who short-changed him two weeks ago, and also the first person to ever give him a piece of salt water taffy. None of this should have been easy to understand, yet all of it was as clear as if he'd read the meaning off a piece of paper.

Max used his fae ability to pale his blush even as it crept up his head. He felt a tiny nudge. Quinn had tapped his foot and was shaking his head with a small smile.

"I've been thinking about something," Quinn said to his mother. "I don't think Lady Time was upset that Farstryke blew up."

"That would make her tantrum rather coincidental," Lady Justice said.

"The thing is," Quinn went on. "I think she moved this

equipment *into* Farstryke. At the same time, they knocked us out and moved us to the street. Lady Time isn't very sentimental—she doesn't really care about Farstryke. I think she was upset about that table and equipment."

Lady Justice looked at Diana. Diana murmured, "That may be quite significant."

"Indeed," Lady Justice said. Then she said, awkwardly, as if *seeing* Quinn, "Your brother will be found. Lord Hermit will commit whatever resources are necessary to mount a search expedition. And if what I heard is true, that includes every resource under Hex, Dagger, and Bone Hollows. And Crusader, of course."

"Lord Magician is helping us?" Max said, surprised. He didn't know Rune had an alliance with him. "I didn't think Rune knew him well."

"Apparently, none of us knew Lord Magician well. Ciaran has claimed the throne. Or was it always his throne? I am confused on that point."

Max and Anna exchanged wide-eyed looks. Quinn made a thoughtful and surprised sound. "That usually only happens in a mountain bar months and months from now," he said, and appeared to find a measure of calm in the stunning announcement.

Then the car was pulling through the gates of Magnus. Lady Death must have been trailing them from above because she swooped earthward and landed in the nearby parking lot for the Chancellor's building.

"We can use a computer terminal inside to pull up Anna's files," Max said as everyone climbed out of the car. "It won't take long. Are we going to Sun Estate after?"

Lady Justice and Diana looked at each other. They shook their heads at the same time. "If you're a target, that's the worst place to go," Diana said. She walked amongst the kids with a critical eye, putting a hand on each of their arms or shoulders. Lady Death did, too, though she added hugs.

Lady Justice said, "I would freely offer my compound as a

safe location."

"Or mine," Lady Death said. "But both may be too obvious."

"We'll consult Lord Tower," Diana said. "He has more bolt holes than a termite. We should hurry."

At this very late hour, the campus was locked down tight. None of the adults seemed too worried about destroying every door or keypad in their way. Lady Justice cracked the defense wards keeping them from the lobby; and Lady Death froze and shattered the locked glass door separating them from the front office.

The Chancellor's offices were ahead in their own suite, set off from an atrium with a two-story glass wall that looked down one of the campus quads. They were primarily academic buildings, empty at this hour.

As they moved toward the corridor to the suite, Max caught a flicker of light out of the vast windows. The glow increased, and a thin line of fire splashed along the distant science building at the other end of the row.

Sound caught up with light, as the base of the science building was sliced from its mooring and collapsed into large, unrecognizable pieces. A silent rush of flames began to consume the pile, and a glowing woman descended to the lawn.

Max and his group watched in shock as she sent another slice of energy against the Mathematics building, slicing it in half and incinerating the remains.

"Diana, call for backup," Lady Justice said and handed her sister her personal phone. "Lady Death?"

"We'll keep her from coming in this direction," Lady Death said to Max.

"Or the other direction!" Quinn cried. "The dormitories are that way!"

"Download the files you need and leave the building," Lady Justice ordered while striding toward an exit. "We'll signal an evacuation alarm. Help will arrive quickly; we just need to keep her at bay."

The Arcana raced for an exit door. Diana touched Max's sleeve and said, "I'll watch from here with Shields ready. Get them to the computers."

Max followed Anna and Quinn at a trot. They'd already run ahead into the suite, and were slapping at computer mice to see which terminals were turned on. There were no others exits in the suite, only windows. Max didn't like dead ends, but at least Diana was watching the hallway.

Since there wasn't anything for him to do, he ran back down the corridor just as there was another tremendous *CRACK.*

Outside the two-story window, they saw the corner of the Culture building begin to buckle and sink. But Lady Time— Max was almost sure the glowing figure had to be Lady Time— was ambushed before she finished slicing through the building. Arms of stone rose from the ground and clamped over her like a giant cupping a bug. At the same time, the lawn around her withered; thick clouds of moisture rose and then solidified, forming a slick ice dome over the stone prison.

Diana pulled a knife from her belt without looking at Max and held it out. Extremely well-crafted metal, and it balanced nicely in his palm.

Outside, stone and ice chunks flew in every direction like mortar fire as Lady Time freed herself.

"I don't think they'll defeat her," Max said worriedly.

"We're just buying ourselves time. We only need minutes."

A desk in the corner of the room shot into the air and catapulted toward Diana and Max. Max barely had time to dive away. Diana, protected partially by a Shield, was knocked unconscious. Max ran over and shouldered the desk off her before Diana's Shield collapsed and she was crushed.

"You've run out of hours and minutes and seconds," Maon said, walking from a shadow. He had a sigil pinned to his chest, a golden sunburst, and what appeared to be Telekinesis swirling around his hands. His eyes were bloodshot, and the veins in his neck popped out like steel wire. He'd injected himself with potions to make him strong and fast again.

Perfect, Max thought.

Maon charged, and Max engaged. He let himself get punched in the face once. As soon as Maon got too sloppy with confidence, Max stopped pretending.

He'd been trained by Brand, and fighting people who were bigger and stronger than you was a first-year exercise. This wasn't a battle, it was a distraction. Now that he knew Maon's battle strengths, it only required a change in tactics.

Four moves later, he ended it by clotheslining the alchemist, who hit the ground with a croak. Max grabbed Maon's head and banged it against the floor several productive times. "You have no idea how good that feels," he whispered to the unconscious fae.

He ran over and checked Diana's pulse—fast but alive. Then a sizzle of energy sounded down the corridor to the Chancellor's suite.

He'd never run so fast in his life. At the doorway, he saw Quinn and Anna huddled on the far side of the main room, with Vadik before them. That's all the time he had before one of the walls was ripped away: a single, flashbulb-quick tableau of Anna's Aspect-bright eyes, Quinn maintaining a smoking Shield before them, and Vadik preparing another fireball.

Then the wall was gone, and fiddle music poured into the room.

Jerica—the principality Fiddler Blue—floated into the room, surrounded by a synesthetic cloud of colorful shapes that were also, somehow, music. Juror Waylan followed her through the jagged hole with a drawn sword.

"Leave them alone," Jerica told Vadik.

"You would betray her?" he spat.

"I have picked a side," Jerica said simply. "And my guess is so will every member of the Revelry after seeing the shit she pulled on that street. She was willing to sacrifice every single one of them just to slow down the Arcanum."

"She'll kill you for this."

"She's not here. You are. And I do not think you want to throw your gifts against mine."

Vadik slapped a hand against his chest and vanished.

"Thought so. We need to run," Jerica said. "She's pursuing you. The Fool told us you'd need numbers. Why did you come here?"

"It's done—we emailed everything," Anna said quickly.

"Is the Revelry alright?" Quinn asked. "Were they hurt?"

"They're fine, thanks to your friends," Juror said. "Gods willing, this will open their eyes about Lady Time."

"I think we have some video clips you'll want to see, too," Max said. "But later. Let's go! Diana is hurt; we need to move her."

The ventilation systems were pumping chemical-scorched smoke into the building as they ran back down the corridor. Quinn and Anna went to Diana while Max ranged ahead to stare out the two-story window.

The haze was nearly impenetrable, but they could see the cratered hearts of burning buildings flaring through.

Then a body crashed against a statue right outside their building, flung from the sky. Max couldn't see who it was—just a plume of pulverized stone. He thought he caught a flash of white leathers.

How did gods fight each other when so much happened at once?

A glowing Lady Time landed gently on the pebbled stone pathway outside the atrium window. The bombardments of ice, fire, and telekinesis stopped. Lady Justice and Lady Death were either down or incapacitated. She walked forward, calmly and unimpeded, straight toward them.

"Run," Jerica said quietly. "All of you run—Juror, go with them! I'll make a stand. We just need to buy time."

Max turned to yell for Anna and Quinn to run and hide, and saw Anna standing there, head cocked to one side. Her eyes were partially closed, as if she was listening closely to something.

"Yes," he heard her murmur.

Fire raced up her body and formed a curving outline above her head, which deepened as more magic fed into it, until revealing itself as a flaming dragon's head. A huge fucking flaming dragon's head. Giant wings unfurled from its lithe, feathered body, and their flap was the sound of thunder. Max stared at it, at *Anna*, with a rush of joy, pride, awe, and worry.

Anna reached up with her hands and *pushed*.

Max felt a torrent of magic sweep past him. The two-story glass window began to vibrate and redden, super-heated. Lady Time stopped her advance to glance up at it—and the entire glass wall erupted into icicle-shaped shards that pelted toward her. She vanished behind a glittering, sharp haze of crushed glass.

Anna stepped forward to stand side-by-side with Jerica. They looked at each other—big, scared eyes meeting big surprised eyes. Jerica finally said, "I have no idea what this is, but if it rolls like a tank, and fires like a tank, then it's a fucking tank. Let's go."

They marched across the lobby and through the broken glass wall.

Outside, the air stank with burnt plastic and wood, the smoke throwing everything beyond fifty feet away into a haze. Lady Time was on her knees, trying to Heal horrific cuts to her face and arms.

"A merry chase," she gasped. "You will pay for every moment of it."

Jerica raised her eyes and slammed a Shield around Lady Time as fiddle music wafted through the air. Quinn circled slightly to her left and threw his own Shield onto hers.

Lady Time's eyes drilled into Jerica. Seeing Juror, too, she added, "All of you."

"You just left them there," Juror spat at her. "The Revelry. You just threw them away on that street like cannon fodder."

"Not *like*," Lady Time said. "And the wonderful thing

about cannon fodder is that they serve a practical afterlife as martyrs."

Jerica held up her phone, which was recording the scene. "I don't think you'll enjoy modern life as much as you think, especially on the city streets. You cannot hide your vulnerable moments—and in that, I include, rather definitively, acting like a raging, narcissistic, lying bitch."

Lady Time lunged. Magic spiraled from her like battering rams, smashing at her containment. Jerica and Quinn both gasped and sank to their knees.

Anna looked plaintively at Max, who swallowed his fear and nodded. Anna reached out to put a hand on Quinn's and Jerica's shoulders. Above her head, the fiery coil of a feathered dragon raised its head to the sky and roared.

Lady Time gasped as the Shield began to thicken and shrink on her. She stopped healing her cuts and put all her effort into breaking free. Sledgehammer thrusts of magic slammed again and again into the Shield.

There was a single second where she stopped and stared, as if surprised. Max finally saw the one thing on her face he'd been looking for on her face: *worry*.

"You do not want to rouse my anger any further today. This is your academy, isn't it?" Lady Time said, her voice amplified with a shaky echo. "I can sense all those young, confused lives. An entire generation of scions nestled in fragile buildings. I will *decimate them*."

She threw her arms wide and screamed. The Shields imprisoning her exploded. Jerica and Anna and Quinn all dropped. A blast radius of fire began burning the grass around Lady Time.

Max had the distinct feeling that they'd run out of road. He pulled the knife from his waistband and saw Juror swing the sword in his hands, warming up. Both began to walk forward, splitting apart into a flank.

That was when a meteor raced across the sky—looking like nothing so much as a mirrored disco ball. It resolved into the form of a man, who landed between them and Lady Time. The walkway asphalt under his feet began to sprout reflective, silvery roses that pushed up through the cracks. The world was subsumed in shades of gray, while everything magical in eyesight began to glow with that reflective light.

Ciaran said, "We've yet to be introduced. I am an adjunct faculty member of these hallowed grounds."

Lady Time laughed at him. "I know who you are. And I can handle all of you at the same time."

"True, but I intend to cheat and activate forty years of charged and recharged mass sigils, primed for defense. Staff membership does have its perks."

He closed his eyes.

The ground began to shake.

Massive layers of Shield began to rise around the buildings, depriving the fires of fuel. Lady Time stared down at her bare foot—just as the flesh began to peel off it. She screamed and fell backwards, and the flesh of both hands, pressed to the earth, began to peel off.

At the same time, figures in robes and battle armor descended around them—Hermit, Strength, and Temperance had arrived at the scene. Lady Death and Lady Justice emerged from the smoke haze, battered and angry.

Lady Time launched into the air with a furious look and fled.

It took Max a good sixty seconds to understand there was nowhere else left to run; nothing else left to find; and no reason to fight.

It was over.

EPILOGUE
Quinn

Quinn was exhausted.

After many, many starts-and-stops to discussions on many, many different issues, the teens were ushered into one of two limos.

Somewhere along the way, Juror and Jerica had slipped away. *That* was a worry for another day. Quinn had no idea what they'd thought of Anna's display of power. She'd used no sigil that people saw—but she had manifested her Aspect. That might confuse Jerica into not realizing…

Well, into not realizing Anna possessed the big secret that Arcana kept, and which no one knew Quinn knew about. And he didn't, not exactly, just enough to prudently keep his mouth shut.

Death and Justice went with them in their limo, and Ciaran rode in the lead car with the Hermit, who had asked him, rather mildly, for *a chat*.

They drove to the Pac Bell first to retrieve Queenie and Corbie. Queenie, carrying the sleeping six-year-old, joined them in the limo. At that point, Lady Death and Lady Justice transferred to the first limo, and the convoy set off again.

Anna was nodding off. She hadn't noticed what Max and Quinn had noticed, which is that, other than the driver, their car was not filled with a single adult fighter. *Why did they…?* That seemed strange.

Then Max stopped seeming worried, and began nodding

off on his own. Quinn thought about waking him up, but he was so exhausted himself.

They all started talking. Sleepily. It was the strangest thing. They talked about lies and white lies, truth and omission. As if they were trying to tell a story in their sleep. Quinn tried to follow the thread of the talk, but it didn't feel like a talk, it felt like a headrush. A massive headrush, like when you stood up too quickly, only this didn't end. Wave after wave of painless disassociation washed over him. He thought, maybe, he was supposed to participate in the talk. Or maybe he was?

It was all so hard to understand, and he was so comfortable. And then…

And then it popped.

Like a soap bubble.

One second, he was in a fugue; the next, he was wide-eyed and alert as whitewater rapids filled his head. It felt so much like his gift, but happiness was outweighed by the fear of what he'd just come to realize, just now, *right now*, as reality rushed back into his mind.

Before him, Queenie had turned to stare out the window. Her fingers idly brushed along Corbie's silky black hair.

But who was Queenie?

Who was this woman opposite him?

How could Quinn have never asked this before? How could he never have wondered what a black hole—a cipher—this person before him was? Why hadn't he seen how unnatural this was?

Where did Queenie come from?

What was her last name?

Did she have parents? Or brothers or sisters?

How old was she?

Who were her people?

How could someone like Queenie exist in their house? A household where everyone lived on top of each other, and knew each other's favorite brand of toothpaste and the way they ate their eggs.

How had no one ever asked? Why would their family—their chronically inclusive family—allow someone to exist in the center of their lives *without being known?*

But she was sitting there. Right there. With Corbie in her lap.

"Puh…" Quinn had to force the word out. "Please give him to me."

Queenie gave him a quizzical look, turning from the window. She saw the expression on Quinn's face. Then she said, in a subtle but rich accent, "Shit."

Queenie shuddered—a full-body shudder. She shook her head, her eyes tightening in discomfort, then sighed as the shaking stopped. It was as if another person entirely was now staring at Quinn.

Queenie-but-not-Queenie said, "I don't think your powers are as permanently lost as you suspect."

"Please give him to me," Quinn repeated, and now he was shaking.

"Young man," she said. "Calm down."

"I don't. I've never seen this. Never. How could I have never seen this?"

"Quite the contrary. Your gift is rather stubborn, and our little chats have become somewhat too frequent. As much as I enjoy them, however, it's not prudent to alter someone's memory this often. Especially memories as important as yours."

"Who are you?" he whispered.

"We have a history, you and I," Queenie-but-not-Queenie said. "I once talked you out of a coma. You called me a nice lady at the time. And I think you'd figure it out if you had time. The name was always a bit on-the-nose." She sighed. "It was too bold a move, giving Annawan the Slate when she left. But it was necessary, and Lord Fool's old vows to me were useful."

She looked out the window once again.

"No more time, I'm afraid. I need to make you forget this moment."

For a crazy half-second Quinn thought about screaming, or clawing a message on his arm, or anyth—

He blinked and yawned. His head jerked up from a nap. Anna and Max were asleep, and Queenie gave him an eager smile.

"I have some peanut butter crackers if you're hungry?" she said.

Corbie muttered and yawned and opened his eyes. "Are we going home?" he asked sleepily. "Flynn doesn't know where I am. He misses me."

"Soon enough," Queenie promised. "Soon enough."

EPILOGUE REDUX
Everyone

The next few weeks were a traumatic blur punctuated by hard milestones.

Rune and Addam returned from the trap Lady Time set. Their triumphant appearance at the Westlands compound ended days when everyone was terrified that they'd been lost.

The Arcanum continued to fight Lady Time, who changed her tactics into hit-and-run attacks against the city infrastructure. The photos and footage that Anna and Quinn had taken turned out to be vital intelligence. Slowly, the picture of Lady Time's robust abilities was shredded. The Hermit's research proved she'd amplified her magic by siphoning her victims' life force, a form of necromancy forbidden since such a distant age that knowledge of it was practically a myth.

Lord Tower was killed protecting Rune and Brand from a near-fatal attack. Vadik was killed. Rune followed Lady Time's desperate retreat, and destroyed her in battle.

Grief was everything for a few days. Everything. The loss of Lord Tower. Of Judgment. The worry over Mayan, and how he'd survive a centuries-old Companion bond. Rune was so weak those first few days after the final battle that he barely functioned for more than an hour between naps.

Rune had also rebranded his court as the Misfit Throne, which a lot of people seemed to like, because suddenly Diana was busy interviewing former Revelry members who were looking for topside jobs. Rune had also opened official talk channels with Juror Waylan and Fiddler Blue, who had claimed their small part of the Eidolon as a compound for the disenfranchised. As gratitude for their role in helping his family, Rune had bequeathed each of them with a sunburst sigil, ones he'd reclaimed from dead Vadik.

There were still certain things the teens promised each other not to tell for now. Or at least certain *nuances* of the truth. Revealing Lord Fool's location? That was fine. Revealing that he'd played a part in bringing Anna to the Eidolon? That wasn't a risk they wanted to take. Until or if Quinn's gifts returned, they were forced to rely on the Fool's warning about future consequences. Any conversation where the Anchorite's name came up bore serious, serious thought.

On a Tuesday not long before the Tower's wake, and shortly after they'd all resettled into Sun Estate, Lady Death picked Anna up in a plum-colored convertible with a tiny shaking dog in a backseat crate.

"You can take her out and hold her if you want," Lady Death told her.

"Brand is watching us from the upstairs window," Anna said. "He's going to text me about seatbelts."

"Then let's make a point of waving at him," Zurah said with a smile.

As Anna opened the crate and cooed at the dog named Ashley, she glanced up. Sure enough, Brand was standing in a second-floor window. A shiny mop of black hair was bobbing up and down at windowsill level. Then Corbie got a good look at Anna holding the dog.

Before he could claw his way through the window, Anna jumped into the front seat and told Lady Death to hit it.

The trip to the Revelry compound involved a lot of roaring wind. The dog stopped shaking and stuck her head out from under Anna's arm so she could lap at the breeze.

Twenty minutes later, they were walking through an abandoned campsite of giant trailer houses—Anna forgot what they were called. Lady Death pointed to a big giant building shaped like a bird, and they walked up that path. Her pocket kept buzzing, which she ignored, because Corbie had already sent thirteen texts.

"This was a nice idea," Zurah murmured. "You have a good heart, Anna. Lord Fool has been... reclusive since his return from the Eidolon. This will do him well."

"Can I ask you something?" Anna asked. "I've been reading some history."

Lady Death gave her a raised eyebrow. Her black braids were adorned with tiny silver skulls with amethyst eyes. "You're about to make me feel old, aren't you?"

Anna, as she usually did when asked rhetorical questions, just waited for the conversation to move on. She wasn't about to tell Lady Death she didn't look old. The woman owned a mirror.

After a few seconds, Zurah threw back her head and laughed. "And a lifelong poker partner is found. What is it you want to ask?"

"About the war. About... The end? What helped end the war?"

Lady Death stepped around a rock sticking out of the well-trod dirt path. "Ah. You speak of Lord Fool and my actions."

Anna had read more about Lord Fool lately. He was a quiet figure in history, but nothing could hide his role in the end of the war. In retaliation for the attack that nearly wiped out dragonkind and made Atlantis toxic, Lady Death and Lord Fool had led targeted, telegraphed strikes in the American Pacific Northwest and Poland. Despite efforts to warn the world of their attack, many died. It turned out to be a decisive moment in the war, and peace talks happened quickly.

"The Eidolon is a ghost trap," Anna said. "Did he build it because of what he did in the war?"

Lady Death considered that for so long, they were nearly at the entrance to the building. "I suspect so. Each of us wears our guilt differently. And he has yet to set his guilt down."

"I don't want to ever feel that guilty," Anna said in a small voice.

Zurah reached out and scratched the head of Ashley, who seemed to be getting excited about her surroundings. She smiled at Anna and said, simply, "Then don't. Make different decisions."

Ashley barked and squirmed out of Anna's arms, and bolted into the bird-building with loud, happy yips. By the time they went inside, the dog was already in Lord Fool's arms, a ball of tiny, bouncing, face-licking fur.

Lord Fool had been alone. The vast, empty building dwarfed the sight of the lone chair he'd dragged into the middle of the floor. After a minute of burying his face into his dog's neck, he blinked and smiled at Lady Death and Anna.

Then he whispered something to Ashley, who barked and leaped out of his arms. She ran around the floor in a widening gyre, and then sprinted for an archway.

"Oh dear," Lord Fool said. "I forgot to put the doggy gate on the tunnel entrance. I don't want her in the Warrens."

"Allow me," Lady Death said. She gave Anna a quick look, inviting her along, but Anna shook her head in an *I'll stay* gesture. "I'll be right back."

"Why haven't you called yet to pick up your dog?" Anna asked when they were alone, because she felt the need to ask *something*. She wasn't very good at small talk. "I know you missed her."

He turned his concussed-pupil gaze away from her. "I'm worried I'll get lost in my head and forget about her. Perhaps you might letter me occasionally to check?"

"Letter you?"

"On the electronic things."

"Oh. Yeah, I can text you. You'll give me your phone number?"

"Of course, dear. But please don't share it with Lord Ciaran. He does love his prank calls." Lord Fool stared in the direction Zurah left. His face was working through the same sort of indecision that Anna's face did. Maybe he didn't like small talk either.

Finally, he said, "You did very, very well, Annawan. I hope you know that. Metaphorically speaking, I expected you to find the little forest path I pointed out, and instead you built an eight-lane highway. But you did get to the right location."

"I had help," Anna whispered.

Now the Fool did look at her. "Indeed," he said just as quietly.

"You know, don't you? What's in my head?"

The Fool took a breath. Then he let it out and took another breath. And then he finally admitted, "I think it best I hold my tongue on that issue. But we only have a minute—Ashley likes being held too much to give Lady Death a long chase. If I told you I would like to help young Quinn, but you must do as I say without asking any questions, would you?"

"Help him what?"

"To, eventually, perhaps, find his way back to his gifts. It is the best path for him. For people like us, our prophecy *is* our normal."

"I would do anything to help Quinn," Anna said seriously.

The Fool pulled an envelope from his pocket. On it was written a single name. Anna's eyes widened in surprise.

Lord Fool said, "Please deliver that in secret. It will put good things in motion."

Anna wanted to ask more questions, but Lady Death was returning with Ashley in her arms.

Plus, the more she got to know Quinn, the more she learned that sometimes, when it wasn't your own battle, it was best to step back and just do what you're told.

She hid the letter addressed to Layne in her back pocket.

On a Friday night, not long after the Tower's wake, Sun Estate held a dinner party, presumably to celebrate Rune and Addam's engagement amongst close friends. Diana had mentioned making the First Friday a tradition—a way to check in on friends and allies. Quinn was doing his best to encourage it, too. In the absence of being able to *See* what was happening, he had to work harder at actually *seeing* it.

The dinner was less napkin-and-silverware and more burger-and-paper-plates, but it was fun and filling, and everyone was glad to keep an eye on Mayan, to the point where he announced actual, real countermeasures to hovering.

Eventually everyone tottered off to digest. Quinn broke away to make some notes in his fake prophecy journal, which he was hoping would trick Anna long enough to find a good hiding spot for his real prophecy journal.

A knock on the door made him look up. No one knocked on doors around here and then waited to barge in.

When he called out, his mother opened the door and poked her head into the room. In a mix of nerves and absurdity, Quinn barked out a laugh.

He slapped a hand over his mouth. "I don't know where that came from."

Lady Justice remained on the threshold. She had on a pair of her indoor sunglasses—the sort of thing she used to keep people from freaking out when her Aspect rose. Not for the first time, Quinn realized what a hard gift that must have been. His mother didn't have nearly as much control over it as she let on.

"Please," he said. "Come in."

She took two small steps into the room, her hands folded before her politely. "I had wanted to attend your event tonight but was waylaid with business. I left a cake downstairs with the boy, if you're hungry. He said he'd bring it to the upstairs kitchen."

Quinn smiled, because she probably meant Corbie, and there was no such thing as a second-floor kitchen at Sun Estate.

"I didn't even know you were thinking about coming. That's really great."

She let the comment sit, pretending not to be looking around his room with interest. As the estate repairs spread throughout the mansion, everyone was slowly moving into their own room, but Quinn and Max usually found reasons to migrate to their old room with bunk beds. This was just the room where he kept most of his stuff.

"It's rare to see you alone without Addam," she said. "You two have been attached at the hip for your entire life."

Quinn's smile dimmed before he could pump more optimism into it. "Do you want me to get him for you?"

"No. No, I wanted to see you. The last time we spoke, I wasn't as aware of the extent of your adventures as I am now. What happened to you in the Eidolon makes for quite the tale. You did very, very well, Quinton."

"Oh mom," he sighed, because he *hated* that birth name.

Her lips twitched. "Your brother, I suspect, has yet to come to terms with your growing sense of initiative."

Quinn shrugged. "I guess. He was very mad I went off on my own."

"As, I've heard, a good parent will," Lady Justice murmured.

She finally walked over and sat in a plain wooden desk chair. Her finger idly drew patterns on the top of his closed laptop. "I would like to say something to you, only I find myself at a loss at how to start."

"Does it help to know I may remember the talk? This isn't the one about me dressing like a page boy, is it? I am really happy at Sun Estate."

Wrinkles spread from her eyeglasses, a rare smile. "I find myself making excuses. But even in my own head, they sound thin and anemic. If it makes any difference at all, there have been moments when I realized how badly I have treated you. There have even been moments I wished I could change it. The love between you and Addam is very special. It warms friends and family alike. But at some point, I realized interfering in your life, at this late date, might do more harm than good. Affecting the growth of a true, strong prophet comes with complications."

"You've known the Fool a while, haven't you? Lord Fool, I mean."

The comment was incisive, and Lady Justice acknowledged that with a nod.

Variations of this talk had played through Quinn's timeline. He didn't understand all of it, but he understood enough. Lady Justice's powers—and the way they worked—had always been a moat between her and other people. She'd seen the worst sides of prophecy and the prophetic gift. She'd lost children in the war. It created a deadly mix for the mother of a sick infant who began showing glimmers of his gift before he even spoke his first sentence.

Lady Justice seemed to weigh all this, even as Quinn did. But the silence between them was too ingrained.

"I will try to do better," she said. "It is not something that can be neatly wrapped with a bow and delivered. For now, I will say that it pains me to hear of these difficulties with Addam."

"He'll forgive me," Quinn mumbled into a shrug.

"Quinn. He already has. This is not a matter of forgiveness. It is not magical, nor Atlantean. It is a reality as old as families. He is watching his child grow up."

Quinn blinked his eyes, and scratched away a tear. "But what if he doesn't like who I'm growing up into? What if he's always mad at me? What if I don't like me, either?"

Lady Justice stared at Quinn for a few seconds. She got up, went over, and, for just a quick moment, laid her hand on his shoulder.

She whispered, "Nonsense, nonsense, and nonsense again."

She left after a few more vague promises to spend time together.

Quinn put aside his fake journal and folded his hands in

his lap, thinking. He wasn't sure he enjoyed that either. *Thinking.* When your thinking was limited to the four corners of your mind—when it couldn't see the sprawl of possibilities flung into the universe by every living, beating heart—it was so lonely.

And then the door burst open, and Addam ran in. He had a stricken look on his face. Addam was a very tall man—with golden hair, a metal hand, and elaborate shoulder tattoos. His strickenness took up a *lot* of space.

"You think I do not like you?" he said, horrified. "You think I will always be mad at you?"

Quinn's jaw sagged. "She did not. Addam, I *just* had a Moment with her!"

Then Addam flew across the room, dragged Quinn to a standing position, and hugged him for a solid sixty seconds. He was crying. Quinn was crying. It was a very messy minute.

"It scares me," Addam finally whispered. "How close you are to the heart of so much danger. It scares me."

"But you're here with me," Quinn said, possibly not as helpfully as he'd planned. "We're all in danger together! That means so much, Addam. You have no idea how much it means, to have as many people as we can on our side."

"You have been unspeakably brave," Addam whispered gruffly. "Never doubt that you are my world."

And then there was more hugging.

Meanwhile, Brand and Max had snuck off to one of the third-floor balconies to have a beer. Or that's what Max thought they were going to do, then Brand started a sentence with "So," which had every alarm bell in Max's head going klaxon.

"So," Brand said. "I've been thinking that maybe it's time to start your training."

"*Start* my training?" Max said. "Because all this has been the kindergarten lead-up? I'll be right back—I need to check something in a safe house on the other side of the world."

"Okay, listen, Rune Junior, calm the fuck down," Brand said, but he was hiding a lip twerk. "I mean training as a team. The three of you. I think you're ready to start training as a field team."

Then Brand looked around him, because the packet of baby carrots he'd laid down were gone. Max and he were sitting at the edge of the balcony, their legs dangling over the parapet. Brand hadn't noticed the ferret sneak forward and drag the carrots into the shadow, but Max had, because it was a ferret. Ferrets must be watched.

"I think it fell over the side," Max said mildly.

Brand shrugged it off and picked up his beer instead. "But seriously. You need the training. While you didn't entirely fuck up on the mission, there's always room for improvement."

Max shrugged.

"I think we need to find a fae fighter," Brand said. "You're starting to find new ways to use your gifts. It's impressive as fuck, and you deserve the best advice. I don't think that's me."

"I have an idea, if you're okay with it," Max said, more than a little nervously. He'd been weighing this in his mind since they left the Eidolon. It felt like a big moment, though, to say the words out loud. He was choosing a path, and it might last his entire life.

"Okay," Brand said slowly.

"Can we see if Ewa Harpur is available? I think I'd like to learn more about battle alchemy." They'd met Ewa, a not-asshole fae, during an alchemy competition.

Brand kept his reaction shuttered. "Why that?"

"Two reasons. One, I think it's a great melee fighting skill. And two, Quinn gets a weird look on his face whenever battle alchemy is mentioned, and tries really hard not to stare at me. I'm pretty sure that's what he thinks I'm going to be."

Brand did smile at this. "Fucking crazy, prophets."

Max smiled, too. "Want to hear a story?"

"I've got two more sips of beer left."

Max took that as a starting signal. "This one time, Quinn and I were at the library. We were walking down a staircase, and I put out my hand to touch the railing. Quinn grabs me and says, *Oh, no. All your timelines go dark if you do that.* And then he goes right back to living his life and trotting off to the next interesting thing, while I stood there with the realization that, at any moment, random shit could spell my doom."

Brand drank the last two sips. He never really laughed, but something about the story amused him. Maybe his moral was, *Now you know my life.*

"They're solid though, right? In the field? It's a good team?" Brand said.

"Wouldn't want another," Max said honestly.

Anna sat on her bed alone.

Rune and Corinne had just left. They'd blindsided her with a Very Serious Talk.

Rune and Corinne had sat on the mattress while she'd sat at her desk. Rune told them both how the Arcana Majeure could one day kill her. Or age her. Or basically mess up her pseudo-immortality.

"I should have told you sooner," Rune had said. He had that angry look on his face that he only used when he was angry at himself. "It's not enough to be told *why* you should be wary of the Majeure. You need to understand its impact on both you and your aunt. And it must remain a secret to anyone who doesn't know."

The Majeure, as Anna understood it, was like a single pool of water. What she used never got replaced. And at some point, all those small uses added up—along with the big ones—and it would make it harder and harder to rejuvenate to an early age. That was what had happened to Lady Time—she'd used so much Majeure to keep herself alive in the timestream that there wasn't enough to rejuvenate her.

He issued a lot of dire warnings. It was a big secret and an implied weakness of Arcana, and they worked really hard to keep people from learning about it. Rune issued so many warnings about using it that Anna was half-worried she should have been writing some of it down.

And all through it, all through the talk, there was that weight in her head. That calm, hissing observation.

Rune left them alone after that. Anna wondered if Corinne would add her own dire warnings, but instead, she leaned close and whispered, "What did it feel like? To use this Majeure?"

Anna, slowly, smiled. "Like I could beat up giants."

"My girl," Corinne said, and kissed the top of her head.

And now Anna was on her bed. Alone. Only it was a very new type of alone. Like the difference between being alone in an empty space, and being alone in a crowd where she was still seen and observed.

After a long time, she got up and went to the mirror on her closet door. She took a few deep breaths and let her magic— her will—raise an amber glow to her eyes.

She said, "I saw you. In my head. For just a second. It looked like you were sleeping in lava."

A flickering snort. In the glass, above her reflection, a snakelike outline formed from invisible steam.

"My name is Annawan Dawncreek," she said.

She heard a sound—a sigh, a small laugh, a curse?

And then the dragon said, *You may call me Kaeru.*

ACKNOWLEDGEMENTS

I'll save a lot of my longer thank yous for the Acknowledgment section in Rune's next book. My apologies in advance to everyone I may have missed here.

This book is dedicated to my beta readers, who really and truly helped get this book to the finish line. What started as a short novella became a short novel—and introduced plotlines and revelations which will fundamentally affect all of New Atlantis. I am so grateful for the beta readers who offered advice, genuine interest, and fellowship.

A huge, huge thank you to the core team behind *The Eidolon*: Danielle and Jamie at Rainbow Crate (check out this amazing, queer subscription book service!); Moon, Michelle, and Justyna; my former agents, Sara Megibow of kt literary and Lesley Sabga of the Seymour Agency; publicist Wiley Saichek of Saichek Publicity; and lawyer Ari Carver.

Thank you to all artists who submitted wonderfully creative ideas for exterior and interior art. I wish we could have included every entry. Particular shout-outs to the artist Oblivionsdream for the cover featuring Max, Quinn and Anna; and Bethany Cath (cheshire.cath94 on Instagram) for the cover of the prophet Quinn. Thank you to Rowan Danckert for the wonderful map. Thank you to Charlie, Michelle, and others who contributed to glossary entries.

Thank you to Ben of TG Geeks Podcast for the constant support, interviews, and announcements. Ben was one of my first interviewers, along with his late, wonderful, very much missed husband Keith. Thank you to the 2022 Cons that meant so much to me during the writing of this book, including ConCarolinas (our contingency keeps getting bigger every year!) and Dragon Con (where I had so much fun with friends, and got to meet one of my heroes, Patricia Briggs, and even saw an amazing Lady Jade cosplay—thanks Rae!).

To Audible for all its support, and especially its amazing, amazing, amazing narrator, Josh Hurley. To Flyleaf, Quail Ridge, Glad Day, and all the amazing booksellers out there who tirelessly support and showcase new authors. And thank you to my much-loved editor at Pyr, Rene Sears. Thank you to all my family and friends, who bravely tolerate me when I'm on deadline.

And, as always, to you. You. Thanks for following Max, Anna, and Quinn on their new adventures.

KD

PS – As I update this Afterword following the first paperback run of *Eidolon*, I'm amazed at how different my life is. I'm now a full-time author with a growing Patreon site and imminent new side content (*The Early Adventures of Rune & Brand*); I'm back to writing at a fast pace again; and I'm nearing the final chapters of the manuscript for Rune's next book, *The Misfit Caravan*. It's been a quiet couple of years, but I intend to surprise and entertain the hell out of you with the remaining seven books in the series. More to come, friend. Be well.

-- K

ABOUT THE AUTHOR

KD lives and writes in North Carolina, but has spent time in Massachusetts, Maine, Colorado, New Hampshire, Montana, and Washington State. (Common theme until NC: Snow. So, so much snow. And now? Heat. So, so much heat.) Mercifully short careers in food service, interactive television, corporate banking, retail management, and bariatric furniture led to a much less short career in higher education, and in 2025, KD achieved his dream of becoming a full-time author. *The Last Sun* and *The Hanged Man* and *The Hourglass Throne* are the first three novels in his debut series, *The Tarot Sequence*. *The Eidolon* now represents a new line of content in the same world.

Please visit kd-edwards.com for a glossary, content warnings, and more. KD has also begun using Patreon as a platform for reader engagement and fresh "between-the-novels" content (patreon.com/c/KDEdwards).

GLOSSARY

World Building

ARCANA. The magically powerful rulers of New Atlantis; inspired the Major Arcana of standard tarot decks. The Arcanum is the highest ruling class of Atlantis.

ARCANA MAJEURE. Very powerful and versatile magic that uses the life force of the user to power and cast a spell instead of a sigil. Considered a secret requirement for an Arcana or principality.

ASPECT. Deep and personal magic, sign of power that takes form based on Court or Personality of the individual. Can evolve over time. Few members of the newest generation have one.

ATLANTEANS. Magical race similar to (and reproductively compatible with) humans.

ATLANTEAN WORLD WAR. Brief human-Atlantean war in the 1960s following the revelation of Atlantis's existence.

CANTRIP. A small, modest magical spell that does not require a sigil.

THE CELESTIALS. The former power bloc of Sun, Moon, and Star Courts.

CONVOCATION. The elected body of ordinary Atlanteans that handles laws and simulates democracy. Does not overrule Arcana.

DRAGON. Magical creature that flies and breathes nuclear fire. Mostly in hibernation post. Atlantean World War, where they were pushed to the edge of extinction. Under triple control of Lord Chariot (strategy and access), Lord Devil (handling), and Lady Moon (caretakers).

ELASMOTHERIUM. A prehistoric rhinoceros, sometimes mistakenly referred to as a dinosaur, that weighs about four tons.

FAE. Magical species that can shapeshift, though not as extensively as Beast throne members. They are creatures of etiquette, and have their own language and unique magical aptitudes. Sometimes called changelings.

FORBIDDEN MAGIC. Includes Weather and Time magic; some of the few magical practices that will result in execution or exile.

GARGOYLE. Magically animated construct created from any object imbued with sentience.

GEAS. A strong compulsion spell that forces the target to follow instructions and rules against their will; resistance or disobedience causes pain or death.

GEREJA AYAM. A building on Lord Fool's property in Squam Swamp colloquially known as the Chicken Church. Translocated from Majelang in Central Java.

GHOUL. Rapidly breeding carnivorous haunts with the faces of mutilated adolescents.

GOLEM. Magically animated construct forged from the deepest fires of the earth and controlled by an activation code.

HALF HOUSE. A nine-foot-wide brownstone, home of the Saint Johns after the fall of Sun Estate and the decade-long protection of the Dagger Throne.

HOUSES (GREATER AND Lesser). Families organized under the sponsorship of Arcana courts.

ICONSGISON. The 22-sided room that serves as the Arcanum's official meeting place.

LICH. The dead soul of a powerful spellcaster who perverted their magic in a hunt for true immortality. The antithesis of existence and Nature; pull the universe into themselves to grow stronger. Appetites have evolved over time from natural disasters to plagues to depravity and atrocity.

LOWLANDS. An area below the Warrens governed by reality-breaking wild magic. Extremely dangerous to enter; it's nearly as dangerous and unpredictable as the Westlands.

MAGICAL DISCIPLINE. A type of magic to which a user devotes years of study in order to perform it without sigils. Certain types of necromancy, plus Frost and Fire spells, are some such magics.

MAGNUS ACADEMY. The elite school for scions that Anna, Max, and Quinn attend.

MASS SIGIL. Overpowered cousin of the standard sigil. A more powerful sigil than a mass sigil is also rumored to exist.

THE MORAL CERTAINTIES. The power bloc of Justice, Hermit, Temperance, and Strength Courts.

NEW ATLANTIS. Formerly Nantucket, an island off America's Massachusetts, the island is now a large city for the surviving refugees of the Atlantean World War.

NULL ZONE. An area of land thought to be devoid of magic. Later revealed to be utterly saturated with magic.

OBSIDIAN. An elemental substance with an adverse effect on magical creatures.

PAC BELL. Property of the Dagger Throne. Formerly the Pacific Bell Telephone building. Lord Tower's private residence spans the penthouse floors.

PORTAL. A magical opening between two locations.

PRINCIPALITY. An Arcana without a Court, with fewer responsibilities and resources.

REJUVENATION CENTER. Two buildings where the Papess Throne practices life. cycle rejuvenation magic. The premier facility is due south of Sun Estate, and built over the last ten years out of healing mud from Italy's Bormio region.

SCION. A member of Atlantean nobility.

SIGIL. An object magically crafted to store spells in for later use. Typically in the form of jewelry or piercings, but also weapons and marital aids. Mass sigils are the more powerful version.

SUN ESTATE. One of the first translocations to New Atlantis. Formerly Beacon Towers, translocated upon its "destruction" in the 1920s by the former Lord Sun.

THE RIVER. A symbolic metaphor for the flow of a person's life, ending where the river meets the unknown sea.

WARD. A magical object with a specific function, such as home defense or allergy prevention.

WARRENS. A mishmash of failed translocations beneath New Atlantis.

WESTLANDS. Poisoned magical backwash of New Atlantis, full of monsters and pocket dimensions. Arcana have compounds built there.

WESTLANDS MORAL CERTAINTIES Compound. The compound owned jointly by the Moral Certainties where Rune battled Ashton Saint Gabriel in The Last Sun.

WESTLANDS SUN COMPOUND. The compound Rune rented out for funds ever since purchasing Half House.

Dramatis Personae

ADDAM SAINT NICHOLAS. Middle son of Lady Justice; second eldest surviving child after the Atlantean World War. Godson of Lord Tower. Rune's fiancé.

ANNAWAN DAWNCREEK. Middle child of Kevan and Mariah Dawncreek. Heir to the Sun throne. Bonded Scion of Corinne Dawncreek.

ANTON SAINT JOSHUA. Lord Tower, Arcana of the Dagger Throne.

BRANDON SAINT JOHN. The lifelong human Companion of Rune Saint John, bonded as babies.

CHRISTIAN SAINT NICHOLAS. Eldest/heir of the Crusader Throne. Married to his Companion.

CIARAN SAINT ANTHONY. Known as a principality of Atlantis; the true Arcana of the Hex Throne.

CORBITANT DAWNCREEK. Youngest child of Kevan and Mariah Dawncreek.

CORINNE DAWNCREEK. Former Companion to Kevan Dawncreek; current Companion of Annawan Dawncreek.

CORNELIUS. A Warrens alchemist. The owl mask of Rune's nine attackers.

DIANA SAINT NICHOLAS. Sister of Lady Justice and caretaker of her children. Seneschal of the Sun throne.

DOMINIKA SAINT NICHOLAS. The Justice Arcana.

ELENA SAINT VALENTINE. Sole and possibly final Arcana of the Lovers court, prior to the raid of the court.

ELLA SAINT NICHOLAS. Third child of Lady Justice. Banished following the events of *The Last Sun*.

FIDDLER BLUE. A reclusive principality who occasionally works with Brand and Rune.

KELLUM GREENWATER OF the Jade Tide School. A merman working in the Green Docks; cousin of Sherman by his father's side.

KEVAN DAWNCREEK. Deceased head of a minor house of the Sun throne. Was bonded to Corinne. Father of Layne, Anna, and Corbie.

LAYNE DAWNCREEK. Eldest child of Kevan and Mariah Dawncreek. Practices necromantic immolation magic.

MARIAH DAWNCREEK. Wife of Kevan Dawncreek and mother of Layne, Anna, and Corbie. Died of health complications many months after giving birth to Corbie.

MATTHIAS SAINT VALENTINE. Nicknamed Max. Grandson of Elena Saint Valentine, ward of Rune Saint John; adopted into the Saint John family at the end of *The Hanged Man*. Parents are alive, but was kept by an uncle. Formerly promised to The Hanged Man for marital alliance.

MAYAN SAINT JOSHUA. The lifelong human Companion of Anton Saint Joshua, bonded as babies.

NATAKI SAINT BRIGID. Lady Priestess, Arcana of the Papess Throne.

QUEENIE. The Saint Johns' housekeeper, who has been with them forever.

QUINN SAINT NICHOLAS. Fourth living child of Lady Justice. A prophet who sees probabilities.

RUNE SAINT JOHN. The last heir of the Sun Throne of Atlantis. Also referred to as The Catamite Prince, The Day Prince, The Prince of Ruin.

VADIK AMBERSON. Youngest son of a former greater house of the Sun throne; the snake mask of Rune's nine attackers.

WARREN SAINT ANTHONY. The false Magician Arcana.

ZURAH SAINT JOSEPH. Arcana of the Death throne. Practitioner of Frost magic discipline.

The Arcanum

0 – THE FOOL
Head of the Revelry Court.

I – THE MAGICIAN
Head of the Hex Court.

II – THE HIGH PRIESTESS
Head of the Papess Throne.

III – THE EMPRESS
Joint-ruler of the Regency; currently in self-banishment.

IV – THE EMPEROR
Joint-ruler of the Regency; the most recent Emperor was killed during the Atlantean War and has not been replaced.

V – THE HIEROPHANT

VI – THE LOVERS
The Heart Throne is traditionally ruled by a pair; no sitting Arcana following a sanctioned raid in _The Last Sun_.

VII – THE CHARIOT

VIII – STRENGTH
Head of the Iron Hall.

IX – THE HERMIT
Head of the Hermitage.

X – THE WHEEL OF FORTUNE
Court ruled by Lord Wheel, who presently resides in America.

XI – JUSTICE
Head of the Crusader Throne; currently held by Lady Saint Nicholas.

XII - THE HANGED MAN
No sitting Arcana following a sanctioned raid on the Gallows in *The Hanged Man*.

XIII – DEATH
Head of The Bone Hollows.

XIV – TEMPERANCE
Head of the Temperance Galley; sometimes referred to as Tolerance (in a bid to disguise KD Edwards's own lapse in memory).

XV – THE DEVIL
Head of the Beast Throne – a court of shifters/weres.

XVI – THE TOWER
Head of the Dagger Throne.

XVII – THE STAR
Sitting head of the Star Court, also referred to as The Anchorite, is imprisoned for crimes against Atlantis.

XVIII – THE MOON
Head of The Nightglade.

XIX – THE SUN
Head of the Sun Throne, renamed the Misfit Throne by Rune Saint John in *The Hourglass Throne*.

XX – JUDGMENT
Head of the Judgment Court; the only heir to the sitting Arcana has been comatose for many years.

XXI – THE WORLD
Head of the Gaia Throne.

XXII – TIME
Arcana of the fallen Hourglass Throne; disbanded for crimes against Atlantis.

www.ingramcontent.com/pod-product-compliance
Lightning Source LLC
Chambersburg PA
CBHW060220180626
46813CB00007B/2895